ALICE
IN
APRIL

ALICE
IN
APRIL

Phyllis Reynolds Naylor

A Yearling Book

Published by
Bantam Doubleday Dell Books for Young Readers
a division of
Bantam Doubleday Dell Publishing Group, Inc.
1540 Broadway
New York, New York 10036

ISBN: 0-440-40944-6

Reprinted by arrangement with Atheneum, Macmillan Publishing Company

Printed in the United States of America

April 1995

10 9 8 7 6 5 4 3 2 1

For Sophia Frances,
the newest member of our family,
with love

CONTENTS

1

WOMAN OF THE HOUSE

It was Aunt Sally who started it. March wasn't even over before I got a note from her reminding me of my birthday in May. As though I might forget or something.

Our little Alice is going to become a teenager, she wrote. Community property, that's me. It was what she said next, though, that got me thinking: *It's a big responsibility, because you're the woman of the house now, you know.*

I guess it was the word *woman* that sounded so strange. Up until then I'd thought of myself as the only girl in the family, but this was different. Woman of the House sounds pretty official.

"What did Sal have to say?" Dad asked as he

divided the mail among the three of us: *The New York Times Book Review* for himself; *Muscle and Fitness* for Lester; and "Occupant" for me. So far that week I'd got a packet of shampoo, a round tea bag, coupons for one free doughnut when I buy a dozen, two packs of razor blades for the price of one, and paper towels at twenty cents off.

"She says I'm Woman of the House now," I told Dad.

"Woman?" said Lester, looking around. "Where?"

Lester is twenty years old and looks thirty because he has a mustache. I'm twelve and look like I'm ten. Sometimes, anyway. It depends on whether you're looking at me sideways or head-on.

"I'm practically thirteen," I told Lester, in case *he* had forgotten.

He gave a low whistle. "I can't believe I've spent more than half my life in the same house with you."

"I can't believe I've spent my *whole* life with *you!*" I retorted.

"Just our luck, huh?" said Lester.

Dad was opening all the bills. "Your mother used to say that if she had to choose two children all over again, she'd take the two she got."

I was a little surprised. "All I can remember is how she used to say we were taking five years off her life."

Dad put down the envelope in his hand. "That

was your aunt Sally, Al"—my name is Alice Mc-
Kinley, but he and Lester call me Al—"Your mother
never said any such thing."

"Sorry," I told him. I always do that. Mom died
when I was little—four, I guess—and Aunt Sally, in
Chicago, took care of us for a time. I can never
remember who was who. I thought about that
awhile, though. "If she wanted me so badly, why did
she wait seven years after she had Lester?"

Dad smiled. "We were waiting for *you*, sweetheart. Babies don't always come right when you
want them, you know."

"I know," I said. I was thinking about Elizabeth's
mother, across the street, who was expecting a baby
in October. Elizabeth Price has been an only child
for twelve years, and she's in a state of shock—
partly because she's about to be displaced, and
partly because anything having to do with bodies
shocks Elizabeth.

I looked at Lester. "When I was born, were you
in a state of shock?"

"Uh-uh," said Lester. "Not till after I saw you.
Then I went catatonic."

I took my mail upstairs and opened the latest
Occupant envelopes. There were coupons for deodorant, sink cleaners, ravioli, and mouthwash. There
was also a little envelope of rich chocolate cocoa,
which I ate with my finger.

Aunt Sally, I knew, collected coupons and kept

them in a little box with dividers in it. I wondered if Mom saved coupons. And then I got to thinking about how, if I was the Woman of the House now, I had to start thinking about things like this. Saving money, I mean. Running a home. Looking out for Dad and Lester. Simply looking after Lester was a full-time job.

I lay back on my bed and stared up at the ceiling. Woman of the House. In charge, sort of. It was weird that all these years I hadn't thought of it once. I'd always felt that Dad and Lester were here to take care of me, but now that I was going on thirteen . . .

I arranged all my coupons alphabetically, put them in a corner of a drawer, and went back downstairs where Dad and Lester were still reading their mail.

"What we've got to start thinking about," I told them, "is spring cleaning."

Dad lowered his magazine. Lester lowered his jaw.

"Cleaning?" asked Dad.

"Clean, as in scrub, sweep, vacuum, and polish?" said Les.

"Whatever," I said. "What we could do is divide up the work."

"I'll dust the piano keys," said Dad.

"I'll rinse out my coffee mug," said Lester.

"I'm serious," I told them. "I don't think we've done any spring cleaning since Mom died."

"Frankly, Al, I don't think your mother ever did any spring cleaning. She vacuumed and straightened up regularly, but I don't remember her making a big deal of spring," said Dad.

"Oh," I murmured. Actually, I was sort of glad, because I didn't much like the thought of scrub-sweep-vacuum-polish either.

If Mom didn't do spring cleaning, though, what *did* she do? Since I didn't much remember her at all, I tried to think about all the women I saw on TV and what they worried about. Toilet bowls. Ring around the collar. Fiber. Dentures.

I was just going to get a pen so I could make a list when the phone rang. It was Pamela Jones, of the long blond hair. So long she can sit on it. At least I thought it was Pamela. It was her voice, but I could hear sobbing in the background.

"Pamela?" I asked.

"Alice," she said. "You'd better come over. I'm here at Elizabeth's."

"What's wrong?"

"Illinois."

"What?"

"Illinois," Pamela said again. "Hurry!"

I grabbed my jacket and went outside. Woman of the House could wait.

2

A TOPOGRAPHICAL QUESTION

The first thing you see when you go in Elizabeth's house is Elizabeth. Above the couch, there's a huge color photograph of Elizabeth in her First Communion dress, with lacy gloves and a veil down the back of her dark hair. She has her hands folded as though she's praying. I suppose she is praying. There's a prayer book in her lap, with white flowers on it.

I asked her once what she prays about, and she said, "Everything." I asked, "What's everything?" and she said she asks God to make her a better person and to protect her mother in childbirth.

I asked Lester once what he prays for, and he said a Porsche while he's still young enough to enjoy it.

Elizabeth's folks were out for the evening, which is why Pamela answered the door.

"Is Elizabeth moving to Illinois?" I asked, looking over at the couch where she lay in a heap.

Pamela shook her head. "Elizabeth *is* Illinois. Come in and talk to her."

Sometimes, when you're twelve, you think everyone else is normal and you're the one who's crazy. Right at that moment I decided that I was normal and everyone else was nuts.

"What is this? A geography assignment or something?" I plopped down beside Elizabeth. She slowly sat up, her eyes red.

"I just found out," she said. "It's the cruelest thing anyone's ever done to me, and I will never speak to a boy again, even if he's the pope."

That was pretty strong for Elizabeth.

Pamela explained: "You know that table at the back of the cafeteria where Mark and Brian and some of the other guys sit? When Elizabeth walked by them today, they called her 'Illinois.' "

I was still trying to understand. "Miss Illinois?"

"J-j-just Illinois." Elizabeth sniffled.

"*So?*"

"Well, Jill called her about ten minutes ago and said that the guys at that table are giving every girl in seventh grade the name of a state. That's why they called Elizabeth 'Illinois.' "

"*So?*" I said again. No one was making a bit of sense.

"Based on the shape of her breasts," Pamela added.

"And Illinois is f-f-flat!" Elizabeth bawled.

It hit me all at once:

1. Seventh-grade boys were staring at our anatomies. One specific *part* of our anatomies.
2. They were talking to each other about us.
3. *I* was going to be named after a state.

I didn't move. I felt as though I had been freeze-dried.

"Listen, Elizabeth." Pamela squeezed onto the couch along with us. "It's really not that bad! There are *some* hills in Illinois, really! There just aren't any mountains, that's all."

Elizabeth sniffled again. "Are you s-s-sure?"

"She's right!" I said. "I used to live there. There are lots of big hills that . . . well, maybe not *big* hills, but . . . more like slopes. Not ski slopes, of course, but well . . . you know those places where the road goes up and down?"

Elizabeth's face was clouding over again.

"Listen," said Pamela. "It could be *much* worse! You could have been Louisiana, you know. Now *that's* flat."

"Or Delaware," I said. "Feel sorry for the girl who gets Delaware."

Elizabeth took a deep breath. "I *still* think they're awful. We don't go around making fun of boys."

Pamela drew up her legs and wrapped her arms around them. "I wonder which state I'll be? Who do you suppose is Colorado? Wouldn't you just love to be Colorado?"

"Jill is," said Elizabeth. "She told me. She's Colorado and Karen's Utah."

I couldn't believe that two of the girls from our old earring club had got two of the best states in the union. I tried to think what state I'd most like to be, after Colorado. I wasn't sure. What state would I most like not to be? And then I knew what would be worse than Delaware: Rhode Island. Not the shape, the size.

I don't pray very often, but suddenly I found myself speaking to God on very personal terms. Dear Jesus Christ, I said. Please let me be anything except Rhode Island.

"What are we going to do?" asked Elizabeth. And then to Pamela, "Can't you talk to Mark?"

"What *can* we do?" asked Pamela. "Knowing Mark, it was probably all his idea."

Elizabeth drew herself up. "Well, I want to name *them* something. I think seventh-grade girls should get together and name boys after the size of *their* things."

Pamela and I exchanged glances. "I don't believe my ears," said Pamela.

"Let's don't talk about it," I quipped, Elizabeth's favorite statement where bodies are concerned.

But this time Elizabeth was so mad we couldn't hold her back.

"*You* know," Elizabeth went on, her face slightly pink. "One boy could be Pikes Peak, and another could be . . ."

We spent the rest of the evening trying to think of a landmark, geographical or otherwise, so small that it would be an insult. The only thing we could pit again Pikes Peak was the Eiffel Tower, but even that would seem like a compliment to a seventh-grade boy. And the parts of our anatomies that boys were talking about were clearly distinguishable, while the part of a boy that we were talking about was not.

"Lester," I said later, "if a girl wanted to really embarrass a boy about . . . um . . . his groin area, what could she say?"

"His *groin* area!" Lester turned and looked at me. "Now, Al, what could a boy possibly do that would make you want to embarrass him like that?"

I told him about Elizabeth being Illinois, and how scared I was I might get Rhode Island.

"Tell you what," said Lester. "If a boy calls you

Rhode Island, say, 'Don't worry; some day the other one will drop.' "

I thought about that a minute. "I don't get it," I said.

"I didn't think you would, so forget it, okay?"

As soon as somebody tells me to forget something, I know I'm going to remember it the rest of my life. So on the bus the next day, I told Elizabeth that if any boy called her Illinois again to her face, she should just say, "Don't worry; some day the other one will drop."

"What?" said Elizabeth.

"I don't understand it either, but Lester says it's the most awful thing you can say to a guy," I told her.

Armed with this new weapon, Elizabeth waited all day for a guy to call her Illinois, and Pamela and I waited to be called any state at all. We saw a lot of smirking and heard a lot of whispering, but none of the boys said anything to us out loud.

That night, I asked Dad what Lester meant by, "Some day the other one will drop."

"Probably refers to the testicles, Al," he said. "Sometimes boys are born with a testicle up in the groin instead of down in the scrotum. In most of these cases it descends soon after birth, but in some boys this doesn't happen until puberty; I'd imagine they're very self-conscious about it."

It was amazing. I had no idea that boys ever had to worry about such personal things. I felt very grown-up, very much the Woman of the House, to know that Dad and I could talk about stuff like this without my passing out on the spot.

I also decided that no matter what a guy called me, I could never say that to him; it was just too cruel. Even if he called me Rhode Island.

3

APRIL'S FOOL

~

Every April Fools' Day, for the past five years, Lester has pulled some trick on me, and I always fall for it.

He told me one April that he'd accidently dropped my toothbrush in the toilet the week before and forgotten to tell me. Another time he said that the FDA had just banned chocolate and no one would be able to buy it anymore. And last year, on April 1, he said he thought I had head lice. Each time I gasped and thought my life was over, and then he said, "April Fool!"

So this year I had it all planned. On the first day of April, I went down to breakfast as usual. Dad and I were eating cornflakes when Lester staggered into the kitchen the way he does in the mornings, his eyes half-closed. Most men shave and shower first, *then* come to breakfast, I'll bet. Lester does it backward. And on this particular morning, Lester groped his way to the table in the Mickey Mouse shorts I'd given him for Christmas, opened the refrigerator, and waited for something to leap out at him.

"Les," Dad said, "will you please choose something and sit down?"

Lester found some cold beans and some bread, and sat down at the table with his head resting on one hand. I think you could say that my brother is definitely not a morning person.

I got up, went to the sink with my dishes, then glanced out the window. I dropped my silverware.

"Lester!" I shrieked. "Your car is rolling backward down the driveway!"

Lester, the Living Dead, leaped to his feet, knocking over his chair. He crashed through the hallway, stubbed his toe on the telephone stand, flung open the door, and hopped out onto the porch on one leg, holding his other foot in his hands.

He came to a dead stop. His car was right where it was supposed to be. A woman across the street, who had come out to get her paper, turned to look at Lester in his Mickey Mouse shorts.

"Al?" said Dad, coming up behind me in the doorway.

I collapsed in laughter. "April Fool!" I shrieked.

Lester wheeled about and hobbled back into the house. "I'll kill her!" he yelled, but I was already halfway up the stairs.

"Al, you're dead meat!" Lester roared.

"April Fool!" I yelped again, barricading myself in my room.

"Road kill!" Lester bellowed, pounding on my door.

I waited in my room until both Dad and Lester had left the house, and then ran down to the bus stop, smirking from ear to ear, and made everyone laugh with my story.

The thing was, though, nobody paid much attention to April Fools' Day at school. Not even Denise Whitlock, the eighth-grade girl who's repeating seventh, did anything awful to me. She's the girl who bullied me last semester, but she just sat staring out the window in language arts, the way she usually does, only half listening.

Back in fifth and sixth, someone was always trying to put something gross in someone else's sandwich, or a boy would try to stick a sign on someone's back that said KICK ME HARD. But April 1 in junior high was pretty much like any other day, and by the time I went home, I was thinking how it wasn't very grown-up of me to go around playing tricks. If I hadn't played one that morning, in fact,

Lester might have forgotten about April Fools' Day this year. Now he'd have some horrible trick waiting for me when I came in.

His car was in the driveway again. I cautiously went up the steps and opened the door. Everything was quiet.

I looked all around and tiptoed out to the kitchen. Lester was at the table eating cheese crackers and reading a magazine. I didn't know whether to step inside or not.

"How ya doin'?" he said. He didn't even look up.

"Okay," I told him, and waited for him to spring—to stick my head under the faucet or something. Nothing happened.

I came slowly into the kitchen and reached for the crackers. Lester didn't even seem to know I was there. I poured some orange juice and sat down across from him. Finally there I was, jabbering away about school, and Lester grunted now and then. I realized what had happened.

Lester must have been half-asleep when he ran out on the porch that morning. That was it. They say that if you wake up after a horrible dream but go right back to sleep again, you won't remember the dream in the morning. Since Lester had never been really awake in the first place, he'd forgotten my trick already. Safe!

I decided to show Dad how grown up I was by

making a salad for dinner—have it waiting in the refrigerator when he came home. I got out the lettuce, carrots, celery, and green pepper, and had just stooped over again to see if we had any onions when Lester said, "Is that the latest style?"

"What?" I said.

"That hole in your pants. Is that how they're wearing them now?"

I bolted straight up. "Where?"

"Right on the seat."

"You're joking!" I said, my fingers searching. "I know you, Lester."

And then my fingers stopped. There *was* a hole! Right on my bottom! A two-inch rip in the seam. I felt my face turn hot. I remembered how I'd had to go up to the blackboard in math, and dropped the chalk while I was up there. Everybody must have seen when I bent over. And in the cafeteria, when I'd put my books under the table, hadn't I heard someone laugh when I stooped over?

"My gosh!" I screamed, and ran upstairs.

I took off my brown pants and threw them across the room. Everybody must have noticed and nobody told me. Pamela and Elizabeth were supposed to be my best friends, and they hadn't said one word. Everybody had let me walk around school with my underwear showing through the hole.

I started to bawl. This was the worst thing that

ever happened to me. This was worse than opening the door at the Gap and finding Patrick, who used to be my boyfriend, standing there in his Jockey shorts. This was worse than accidently kicking one of the sixth-grade teachers during a Halloween parade.

This would follow me all through eighth grade, ninth, and senior high school—the girl in the Fruit of the Loom pants. I sobbed.

Lester came to the door of my bedroom. "For Pete's sake, Al, April Fool!" he said.

I grabbed the bedspread and wrapped it around me. "You're just saying that! There really *was* a hole in my pants!"

"Relax! If there was, I didn't see it," he said.

I gulped. "You didn't? Lester, tell me honest and truly: Did you see a hole in my pants or not?"

"Of course not."

"Well, I think it's really strange that you just happened to pick that as an April Fool joke when the hole was really there."

"Coincidence, Al."

"You're just trying to make me feel better."

"Why should I want you to feel better after what you did to me this morning?"

He remembered! "Are you sure you didn't see the hole in my pants first and then think of the joke?"

"Arrrggghhh!" cried Lester. "Okay! Okay! Let's

say I did see it. Have it your way. If that's the most embarrassing thing that ever happens to you, you're one lucky kid." And he went back downstairs.

I sat woodenly on my bed. Did he mean that far *worse* things were ahead? Did he mean I'd go to school someday with a hole in the seat of my pants and not have underwear on at all?

I pulled on a pair of jeans and went downstairs.

"Lester," I said, "if you wake up some morning and I'm not here, you'll know I've hitchhiked to Alaska."

"Have a nice life," he said.

4

THE SEWING LESSON

I decided to mend the rip in my pants, and after that, I'd check all of Dad's and Lester's clothes for rips or holes or buttons that were missing. But first I called Aunt Sally.

"I'm mending," I told her.

"Good!"

"I don't know how."

"Alice McKinley!" she scolded. "Are you telling me you're almost thirteen and you don't even know how to stitch?"

"I guess so," I said.

She told me how to make a knot in my thread and run my needle in and out along the seam where the stitches had come loose.

It sounded simple enough, so I got out the sewing basket, found some dark brown thread, and did what Aunt Sally told me.

It occurred to me that in all the years I'd been coming to this basket to get safety pins, I'd never really stopped to think that this sewing basket had probably belonged to my mother. She used to hold the scissors just as I was holding them. She'd picked out every spool of thread. I swallowed. I figured she would have been pleased to know I was learning to be Woman of the House for Lester and Dad.

I wore my brown pants to school on Monday, and was glad I'd mended that hole, because just after lunch, as I walked by the table of seventh-grade boys at the end of the cafeteria, I heard one of them say, "Florida."

I didn't turn around but my pulse beat like crazy. Were they talking about me? Was that who *I* was going to be? Was Florida better or worse than Delaware? Better or worse than Louisiana? Better or worse than Illinois?

"Patrick," I said in gourmet cooking, as we stood at the stove together, stirring our lemon custard. "You know how those guys in the cafeteria are naming girls after states?"

"Yeah?"

"Could you do me a big, big favor? Could you

find out what state they're planning to name me?"

Patrick stuck one finger in the custard and licked it. "Which state do you want to be?"

I looked at him in delight and wonder. "You mean I could choose it myself?"

"Why not?"

"I can choose any state I want, and you'll suggest it to the guys?"

"Sure."

For the first time in my life, I saw the need to study geography. All those years back in fourth, fifth, and sixth, why couldn't I have paid more attention? Did I want mountains or did I want hills? Would I rather be desert or wetlands? Which were the timber states and which were coal? Each little feature was enormously important.

I realized that my ignorance of geography could affect my entire life. If I chose a flat state by mistake, I could get a nickname that would follow me through college. If I was Delaware, for example, every inscription in my senior yearbook would be something like, *Good luck, Delaware Al! Hang in there, Delaware!*

It was more responsibility than I could handle. I wanted someone more knowledgeable than me to pick my state. So after the custard had thickened and we were dividing it into dessert dishes, I said, "Patrick, I want you to pick a state for me and suggest it to the guys. Will you?"

"I guess," said Patrick. Just like that.

The day seemed to creep along and I could scarcely wait till we got on the bus again so I could find out what state Patrick chose. In language arts, Miss Summers, who dates my dad, asked me what poem by Carl Sandburg described a city, and I said, "Illinois" instead of "Chicago." The boys laughed.

Maybe I should have asked Patrick to call me the name of our own state, Maryland. Maryland had everything, from mountains to ocean, so wouldn't I be safe with that? Then I wondered if Maryland had something awful I didn't remember. No, the more I thought about sending Patrick to make a suggestion, the more I decided it was a stroke of genius. Not only would he make a better choice, but I'd know what he really thought of my figure, how *he* saw my body.

As we got on the bus that afternoon, Pamela and Elizabeth sat together, so I slid onto the seat beside Patrick before any of the guys could sit there.

"Well?" I said.

"What?" asked Patrick. The thing about boys is they take so long to catch on.

"Which state did you choose?"

"Oh, that," said Patrick. "Maine."

I stared. Somehow I had been thinking California. West Virginia, maybe. *"Why?"*

"What do you mean, why? Because Dad and I went float fishing there once, and I liked it."

"I'm going to be called Maine the rest of my life because you liked float fishing?"

"Seemed like a good reason to me."

"Patrick, think!" I cried. "Does it have any hills and valleys?"

"I don't know. We were along the coast."

I slid down in the seat. Patrick could have called me California. Montana! New Hampshire, even!

"Patrick, the guys name girls after states depending on their *figures,* not float fishing."

"But that's dumb, Alice. I liked Maine," he said. "What do you care, anyway, what a bunch of guys call you?"

I didn't answer. I could feel my eyes welling up and was afraid I'd bawl.

"Besides," Patrick went on, "they already had a Maine, so that's not you."

I thought I'd lose my mind. I bolted straight up and grabbed his arm. "What state *am* I, then?"

"I don't know," Patrick said. "It was between Florida and some other state, but I can't remember which."

Pamela and I decided that not knowing was the worst. If you were Rhode Island, even, at least you'd know that all the dreams you'd had for junior and senior high school were gone forever, and you could look forward to becoming nothing more than a check-out clerk at the Safeway or something.

After I got home, however, I discovered what was worse even than that. The hole in the seat of my pants was back again. My stitching hadn't held. I had been going around school all day with my underwear showing, and the kids who hadn't noticed it the first time would surely have noticed it the second.

I don't know what it was about seventh grade, but I felt even less confident of myself than I had in sixth. I couldn't seem to do anything right. Couldn't even sew up a two-inch rip in my pants.

Dad must have noticed my red eyes when he got home because he asked what was wrong.

"Nothing," I said.

"Nothing you want to tell me, you mean," he insisted.

So I told him how I'd followed Aunt Sally's instructions, but that the stitching hadn't held.

"Did you secure the thread when you finished— tuck it in good and tight so it wouldn't work loose?" he asked.

"No, I just cut it."

"Go bring me the sewing basket," he said.

Dad and I sat at the table together and I watched while he sewed up my brown pants.

"I didn't know you could do that!" I said in astonishment.

"Who do you think has been mending your clothes all these years?" he asked.

I hadn't given it much thought, actually. The

elves, maybe. All I knew was that after I'd been wearing safety pins in my clothes for three or four
months, I'd put them in the hamper one day, and
when I got them back, they didn't have pins anymore.

"Did Mom teach you to sew?" I asked when he
showed me how to knot the end of the stitching.

"No, but after she died, I learned in a hurry," he
said.

Lester came in and got a soda out of the refrigerator, then watched the sewing lesson. I was even
feeling kind toward Lester. Now that my pants were
mended, I realized I had a reason to live. Then I
remembered how Patrick could have called me California, but didn't, so I might be Florida.

"Lester," I said, "what's the first thing you think
of when I say 'Florida'? About the land, I mean?"

"Sinkholes," he said.

I stared. "Sinkholes?"

"And swamps," Lester added.

I ran upstairs to spend the rest of my life in my
room.

5

FAMILY BUSINESS

Sometimes I think my life would be simpler if I didn't have any aunt in Chicago. Aunt Sally is my mom's older sister. She's married to Uncle Milt, and they have a daughter, Carol, who's a few years older than Lester.

I guess it's because Aunt Sally can't quite believe we're still alive after Mom died that she calls so often to find out if we need her. She can't believe that my growth hasn't been stunted, that Lester's not on drugs, and that Dad hasn't married "the first floozy who comes along," as she puts it. To Aunt Sally, it's a "wondrous amazement" that we function as well as we do.

"Alice," she said when she called that evening.

Lester was out, and Dad had gone back to work to put in a few more hours. I was the only one home. "Have you decided yet what you want to do with your life?"

I didn't even know what socks I was going to wear the next day, and Aunt Sally wanted to know what I was going to do with my life.

"Not really," I told her.

"Well, one of these days you'll have to start choosing your course of study. You don't want to wait until the last minute, then find out you have to have chemistry in order to be a surgeon or something."

"Aunt Sally," I said, "the only way I would ever become a surgeon is if someone threatened to kill me, my family, and wipe out the North American continent unless I did."

"A pharmacist, then." Aunt Sally just wouldn't give up.

"What was Mom?" I asked her.

"Your mother was a homemaker, Alice, one of the most noble professions there is, and if that's your choice, I won't say a word against it."

The word *homemaker* always throws me. It sounds as though homemaker is what you have to have if you want a home, yet Dad and Lester and I seemed to get by, and there was no homemaker here that I could see.

I asked Aunt Sally about it, and she said a homemaker just makes a *better* home, that's all.

"But what does she *do*?" I wanted to know.

"A lot more than dishes and dusting," Aunt Sally
said, "In addition to keeping the house clean, the
clothes mended and pressed, and food on the table,
a homemaker is aware of the seasons. She puts away
winter clothes in the spring, summer clothes in the
fall, airs the pillows, dusts the blinds, cans the veg-
etables, preserves the fruit, and turns the mat-
tresses."

I swallowed.

"And that's only the house," she went on. "The
most important part of her job is people. A homemaker is a nurturer, Alice. She knows what each
person in her family needs, who will be working late,
who will be rising early, who needs a sack lunch,
who needs a light supper, and she remembers all
birthdays, music lessons, and dental appointments."

I felt as though I should be making a list.

"Well, I just haven't decided yet what I want to
be," I said again. And then, because I didn't want to
sound like a total loser, I added, "Right now the
choice is between a chef, a waitress, and a forest
ranger." I realized after I'd said it that two out of
three had to do with food.

There was a long pause at the end of the line.

"Hello?" I said.

"Alice," came Aunt Sally's voice, "a chef and a forest ranger I can take. But let me tell you what you have to look forward to if you become a waitress: tomato stains on your uniforms; varicose veins; customers who don't know the difference between sunny-side up and over light; and," she added darkly, "men who want to drive you home."

By the time she got to the end, I'd forgotten whether these were pros or cons.

"*I* was a waitress one summer when I was in my twenties," Aunt Sally went on, "and every day this man came in for lunch, and when I'd ask him what he wanted, he'd look me up and down and say, 'Nothing that's on the menu.' " She stopped so that I could get the full import of what she meant.

"If you decide to become a waitress, Alice, I want you to promise that if a man ever says to you, 'Nothing that's on the menu,' you'll go get the manager."

"Okay," I said.

When Lester came home, I asked, "Les, did you ever say to a waitress, 'Nothing that's on the menu'?"

Lester sighed and took off his jacket. "I've had a rough day, Al. What are you talking about?"

I told him what Aunt Sally had said.

"I haven't yet," said Lester, "but I'll keep it in reserve."

Something Aunt Sally said, though, about birthdays, got me thinking. Usually I don't remember anyone's birthday but my own. I'll remember Dad's or Lester's when I write the date on a math assignment, maybe, and then I'll go over to the Giant after school and buy a decorated cake from the bakery, the kind Dad scrapes all the roses off of first.

Dad, on the other hand, remembers both Lester's birthday and mine in advance, always has a present waiting, and usually asks me a week or two ahead of time where I'd like to go for dinner.

The Woman of the House was supposed to remember things like this. I went right to the calendar Dad keeps above the telephone and circled two birthdays—Dad's, on April 30, and Lester's the fourth of September.

"Dad's birthday is coming up the end of this month," I told Lester. "How old is he going to be?"

"The big five-o!" Lester said.

I stared. "Fifty?"

"You got it."

I couldn't believe it. My dad, half a century old? Some people died when they were fifty! You were supposed to have false teeth and fallen arches when you were fifty! And then I remembered something else Aunt Sally said—that a homemaker keeps track of everyone's needs. How was my dad's health, anyway? Did he have any needs I should know about?

When the phone rang again, I figured it was Aunt Sally with still another idea to add to my homemaker's list, but this time it was a younger female voice: "May I speak with the woman of the house, please?" she asked.

"I'm the woman of the house," I said. From across the room, I could see Lester rolling his eyes.

"I'm calling to see if you would be interested in a five-hundred-dollar certificate toward family planning," the voice said.

My first thought was that a five-hundred-dollar certificate would make a fantastic birthday present for Dad; my second thought was that planning a birthday party was not what the woman had in mind; my third thought was that this had something to do with birth control, and I'd better put Les on the line.

"Um . . . what kind of planning?" I asked.

" 'A happy family is a prepared family,' we say in this business, and I wonder if you already have your cemetery plot."

Someone *else* knew my dad was going to be fifty!

"Well . . . uh . . ." I thought of all Dad's relatives down in Tennessee and figured there must be a plot down there somewhere. "I think we already have a family plot," I told her.

"Then you could apply the certificate toward a gravestone. A number of families have plots, but few have thought of the expense of a gravestone. Ordering one in advance would save the family an added burden at a trying time."

"I don't think we're in the market for a grave-stone," I told her. I could see Lester's eyebrows go up.

"The five hundred dollars could also be applied toward a casket," the woman told me. "Do you have a casket?"

"A casket?" I croaked. "Where would I put a cas-ket? I don't think I'm in any hurry to run right out and buy one."

"Well, not today, perhaps, but tomorrow or the next day," the woman said.

I finally had to hang up on her. She just wouldn't quit. Lester said the next time the cemetery-lady called, I should tell her that we planned to be cre-mated and float our remains down the Potomac. But I began to worry again about Dad.

The next day I stopped by the Melody Inn Music Store, where Dad is manager, to see if there were any new earrings in the gift section. Dad's assis-tant—Janice Sherman, in sheet music—happened to mention that Dad needed a vacation.

"He's working much too hard," she said. "I was here filling orders until ten last night, and he was still working when I left. Maybe you and Lester could talk him into taking some time off."

"I'll see what I can do," I promised.

The person I should talk to, I was thinking, was my language arts teacher. Maybe I could suggest that she and Dad take a long weekend together, but Lester nixed that idea.

"First of all, the idea should come from them, not from you," he said. "In the second place, Dad's much too straight to go off for a weekend with a woman he's not married to."

"Why not? They don't have to sleep together," I said.

"Well, things don't work that way, Al. Even if they had separate bedrooms, people would *assume* they slept together."

"That's stupid!" I insisted. "That's just plain dumb! Besides, why do they care what other people think as long as *they* know the truth?"

As soon as I'd said the words, I remembered what Patrick had said to me about why should I care what state a bunch of boys named me. But it didn't seem quite the same, somehow.

"Dad," I said later that evening as he sat down to play the piano. "Don't you think we should have a family doctor, and go for checkups and everything?"

"Actually, I was thinking about that myself last week, Al," he told me. "If one of us should get really sick, we need someone we can call. So I made appointments for all three of us to have physicals."

Physicals? All? We, me included? A "physical" sounded a lot more serious than a checkup.

"I meant . . . uh . . . you and Lester," I told him.

"It would be a good idea for *all* of us, sweetheart. It's been a long time since any of us had a really thorough exam. Your body's changing, and I want you to have someone you can go to for personal questions, in case you feel you can't ask me."

I didn't want to see a doctor. More to the point, I didn't want a doctor to see me. "I can't think of any questions I couldn't ask you," I told him.

"But one day you might, and I want someone to be there for you," he said. "You and Lester have appointments on Thursday afternoon. I've arranged it so you can go together."

"In the same room?" I squeaked.

"Of course not, Al. One at a time."

"I'm healthy as an ox," Lester said.

"Well, I want to keep you that way," Dad told him. "I'm going to have a doctor check you both over from head to toe."

I gulped. "Naked?"

And when Dad nodded, I realized it didn't matter whether the boys called me California or Rhode Island, because even Colorado would be embarrassed to stand in front of a doctor without her clothes.

6

HUMILIATION

I didn't tell anyone where I was going on Thursday. Pamela asked me to come over after school, and I just said I had to go somewhere with my brother. When I got home I put on clean underwear, washed my feet and armpits, and brushed my teeth. Then I put on a blouse and skirt and went out to the car where Lester was waiting.

That morning, to make me feel better, I guess, Dad had told me I'd be seeing a woman doctor. It helped some, but not a lot.

"Have you ever had a complete physical?" I asked my brother. "I mean, *every*thing?"

"Sure," he said, backing down the drive.

"What's it like?"

"Well, first they take this four-inch-long needle and stick it in each eyeball. Then . . ."

"Lester, stop it."

"It's really not so bad, Al. Builds character! The only part I don't like is when everyone has to line up naked to be weighed."

"Everyone *together*?" I shrieked.

"Just kidding. Truthfully, if you can get through the specimen process, the rest is a piece of cake."

I didn't know whether to trust him or not. "What's the specimen process?" I asked warily.

"When the nurse holds a paper cup under you and asks you to pee."

I put my hands over my ears. "I'm not listening. Shut up! Just shut up!"

We must have looked weird walking in the medical building, me with my hands over my ears humming as loudly as I could so I wouldn't hear anything Lester said.

A. J. RICHARDS, M.D.; M. P. THORNTON, M.D.; R. B. BEVERLY, M.D.; INTERNAL MEDICINE, it said on the door.

Lester and I went in and sat down. He picked up a copy of *Sports Illustrated*. I picked up *Better Homes and Gardens*, but I didn't read a word. I was too nervous. This didn't look at all like the pediatrician's office back in Takoma Park with clowns and elephants on the walls.

The receptionist gave us each forms to fill out, and Lester did mine for me.

"Ever had mumps, chicken pox, or measles?" he asked me.

"How should I know?" I said.

He put question marks in the spaces.

"How about mental illness. Check yes?"

I gave him a look.

Finally the nurse said, "The McKinleys?" And when we nodded, she said, "Alice, will you come with me?"

I followed her into the back hall. Whatever horrible thing was about to happen, I wanted to get it over with.

"Let's see. . . ," the nurse said. "You're here to see Doctor . . . ?"

"Beverly," I told her.

"Okay." She handed me a paper cup. "If you'll just take this to the restroom around the corner and give me a specimen, I'll take it when you're finished."

Ha! I thought. I'd never listen to Lester as long as I lived. When I came out of the restroom, though, I forgot which way to turn, and found myself in the waiting area again. Lester was engrossed in his magazine, and there was only one other person in the room.

As I passed, I nudged Lester. "Want some lemonade?" I asked, holding out my cup, and he almost took it.

"Al!" he said suddenly, glaring at me, and I laughed right out loud.

The nurse was watching us from the doorway. "Brother and sister?" she asked when I came back in. I nodded.

She weighed me, took a blood sample, then my blood pressure, and finally led me to a room with a desk and chairs in it, and a wall full of books. "The doctor will be with you shortly," she said.

There was a picture of Dr. Beverly and her two children on the desk. She was a gorgeous brunette with large white teeth and beautifully shaped eyebrows. I was just settling down to read the titles of all the books when a man walked in and put out his hand. "Hello, Alice. I'm Dr. Beverly," he said, and sat down.

I was too astonished to speak; too amazed to tell him he had the wrong patient. I had been so sure that the female of the four was Dr. Beverly that I hadn't even thought to ask. But now that he was here, how could I say I didn't want him? I thought of saying, "I thought you were a woman," but that didn't sound right either.

What I said was nothing. What I did was nothing. I just gave him a little smile and went on digging the fingernails of one hand into my arm.

"Well, how are we doing?" he said. "Is something in particular bothering you, or are you just here for a tune-up?"

I figured that any doctor who referred to a physical exam as a tune-up couldn't be too bad, so I decided to stick with Dr. Beverly. He asked questions about my family, and I told him how Mom had died of leukemia when I was four. We had just got to how often did I have sore throats or earaches when I heard Lester's desperate voice out in the hallway.

"I'm sorry, sir," the nurse was saying, "but Dr. Beverly is with a patient."

"I understood I'd be seeing a male doctor," Lester said.

"Dr. Richards is an excellent physician. I think you'll like her, but if you'd prefer to wait for Dr. Beverly, he could see you in an hour, perhaps."

Lester mumbled something I couldn't understand, and their footsteps faded away. I decided to stay right where I was and let Lester see the woman doctor. It would be good for his character.

When we were through with the talking part, Dr. Beverly rang for the nurse and she took me to an examining room.

"Now," she said cheerfully, "I want you to take off all your clothes except your slip. Are you wearing a half slip?"

I nodded.

"I always let patients keep on a little something of their own," she whispered with a wink. "Makes them feel more secure."

I didn't tell her that I wouldn't feel secure if I were surrounded by the United States Army.

"Then," she went on, handing me a paper sheet, "put on this robe, with the opening in front, and climb up on the table." She went back out and closed the door.

Robe? I unfolded the paper sheet. There were two holes in it for my arms and a string to tie it around me. I looked at the door and then at the robe. How long before they came back? What if I got all my clothes off and they came in before the robe was on?

First I took off my shoes and parked them under a chair. Then I took off my blouse and bra and hung them on the back. I slipped my arms into the robe to cover me, then took off everything else. I tied the string into a triple knot.

Saved! I stepped up on the stool and then onto the table. Yikes! My bra and pants were showing! I slid off the table and stuffed them into one shoe, then climbed back up again.

Everything in the room looked scary—the strange assortment of instruments on a paper towel; the syringes on a stand; the rubber gloves; the flexible light. . . .

It was weird, but I suddenly thought about Mom just then—wondering if she'd been sitting in a doctor's office in a paper robe like this the day she found out she had leukemia. Was Dad waiting for her out in the reception room, or was he with her? Did the doctor tell him first, or tell them both together? Maybe someday I'd ask.

There was a light tap on the door, and then the doctor came in, the nurse behind him, holding a clipboard. Dr. Beverly washed his hands at the sink.

"Now let's take a peek and see what's what," he said. I hugged the robe even more tightly to my body.

The peek he had in mind, though, was in my mouth and ears and nose. He turned off the overhead light and shone a flashlight in my right eye, putting his face up close to mine. I kept my lips tightly shut in case I had bad breath. Then he moved to the other side of me and looked into my other eye. Every so often he said something to the nurse and she wrote it down.

The overhead light came on again and Dr. Beverly pressed his fingers along the sides of my neck. Then he told me to take deep breaths while he listened with a stethoscope—first my chest, then my back.

The nurse pulled out an extension at the bottom of the table and asked me to lie down.

Here it comes! I told myself, and shut my eyes.

"I'm going to examine your breasts, Alice, then your tummy. If anything hurts, be sure to let me know," he said.

It was the first time a doctor had ever acknowledged I had breasts. My old pediatrician had always referred to my "chest." What if Dr. Beverly looked under the paper robe and said, "Are these supposed to be breasts?" or, "Nurse, this girl has no breasts!"

He opened the top of my robe and folded back one side of the paper gown. He pressed his fingers in a circle all around the edges of that breast, and all the while, he was talking:

"I've got two girls of my own, nine and eleven. Both of them are into soccer. Do you play soccer, Alice?"

He was examining my breasts and talking soccer? I think I loved Dr. Beverly.

"Uh-uh," I said, my eyes still shut.

"Me either," he told me. "Sure did have to learn about it in a hurry, though, when the girls joined teams."

He covered that breast up again, then did the other. Maybe this wasn't so bad, I thought. I opened my eyes just a little, and then they popped wide open, for there on the ceiling above the examining table were cartoons about doctors and patients! Other people had lain here just like me and lived. Other people had read those cartoons.

"Breasts normal," the doctor said, and the nurse wrote it down.

Normal? My breasts were normal? I couldn't believe it. Was normal the same as average? Neither

Colorado nor Illinois, but somewhere in between? I was feeling much, much better when he said, "Now your tummy," and I realized he was working his way down. First the eyes, then the neck, then the breasts, the tummy, and then . . .

Something was wrong. Something was happening! He wasn't examining my stomach! And then I realized that Dr. Beverly was trying to untie the knot in my string. *Why*, why hadn't I tied a bow? The nurse finally handed him the scissors from the tray, and the doctor had to cut it. Neither of them said a word. I closed my eyes again.

"Tell me if any of these areas are particularly sensitive," the doctor said, and the five fingers of his right hand pressed here and there. Nothing hurt.

As soon as he'd covered me up again, he said, "Any problems in the pelvic area, Alice? Pain? Discharge or itching?"

"No."

"Menstrual periods okay?"

I nodded, my hands gripping the edge of the table as though it were a rocket about to blast off.

"Fine. Then I don't think I need to check you there," he said. "You can sit up now."

I blinked. This was it? The worst was over?

"Let me check your knees," Dr. Beverly said, and after tapping each knee and making my feet jump, he checked my spine to make sure it was growing straight, and then it was done.

"You're a perfectly normal twelve-year-old, Alice—woops, almost thirteen," he said. "Everything seems right on target here, your height, your weight. . . ."

The nurse smiled and left the room.

"Is there anything else you'd like to talk about?" Dr. Beverly asked. "If you're anything like my own two girls, you've got a lot of questions."

I tried to think. Now was my chance. Wasn't there any deep, dark question so embarrassing I couldn't even ask my dad?

"When am I . . . well, officially, I mean . . . a woman?"

Dr. Beverly just smiled a little and looked thoughtful. "Well, I know some women of eighty who act like girls, and some girls of eight or nine who act like old ladies. So I can't really say, Alice. When you *feel* like a woman, I guess you are."

He left the room, and I did my quick-change act again, in case the nurse forgot something and came back. When I was dressed, I went out into the reception room to wait for Les.

He came at last, looking like a man who has just been examined by a woman doctor.

"Let's go," he said, not even looking around, and didn't talk all the way back to the car. I could hardly keep up with him.

"Are you okay, Lester?" I asked finally as he turned the key in the ignition.

He grunted.

"Did it hurt?" I asked.

"Only my pride," he answered.

It wasn't until later, when I heard him telling Dad how he'd got a young redheaded woman doctor, that I figured what the problem was: He had gone for his checkup in his Mickey Mouse shorts.

7

LOOKING AHEAD

~

The next day at school, I seemed obsessed with bodies and physical exams and just exactly what it meant to be a woman. In language arts, I couldn't help staring at Miss Summers, with her light brown hair and blue eyes, wondering how many times she'd had her breasts examined and if you get used to it after a while.

She was wearing a silky peach-colored blouse with silver buttons. The fabric hung in soft folds, and the embarrassing thing was I couldn't keep my eyes off her bosom. I decided I wanted breasts just like that when I was grown—not too big, not too small, about the size of tennis balls, I guessed. Yes, that was it exactly. I'd wait till my breasts were the size of tennis balls, and then I'd bind them up at night so they wouldn't grow any larger.

When the bell rang, I went up to Miss Summers's desk to turn in my paper.

"I wasn't sure you were with us this morning, Alice," she said. "Your mind seemed a million miles away. What were you thinking about?"

"Tennis," I told her. And then, embarrassed that my eyes were on her breasts again, I said quickly, "I like your buttons."

"Thank you," she said.

Pamela and I went to Elizabeth's to spend the night, and I told them all about the physical exam with Dr. Beverly. Just as I got to the part where he peeled off the paper robe as though he were unwrapping a ham sandwich, Elizabeth said, "I don't want to hear about it."

"Yes, you do," said Pamela. "You always say that, Elizabeth, but you want to hear about it as much as I do."

Elizabeth's eyes grew wide. "Pamela!"

Pamela barrelled on. "If you can't talk about things like this now, how are you ever going to get married and have children?"

"I don't know!" Elizabeth wailed. "What I can't stand is that . . . well, all the things you talk about with your mother now, you'll have to talk about with a man someday."

Pamela shrugged. "So talk! What's so hard about that?" She looked over at me and her eyes were laughing. "Marvin," she said, imitating a grown woman. "Would you go to the store and buy some Kotex for me?"

"Stop it!" said Elizabeth, but we continued.

"Light, medium, or super?" I asked.

"Super plus," said Pamela.

"I mean it, you two!" warned Elizabeth, her face reddening.

"Deodorant or unscented?" I asked.

"Something that smells like rose petals," said Pamela.

"Extra long or regular?"

"I'm going to leave if you don't stop right now!" Elizabeth cried, standing up.

"You can't. It's your house," I told her. "Elizabeth, your husband has to tell you embarrassing things too. What if he wanted you to go to the store and buy a new jockstrap for him?"

Elizabeth sat back down. "A what?"

"A jockstrap. To keep his . . . *things* in," Pamela told her, giggling.

Elizabeth looked puzzled. "You mean shorts? Jockey shorts?"

"No, a little sort of harness he wears when he's playing basketball or something," I told her, remembering when I'd seen Lester's in the wash. "So he won't bounce around."

"I *wouldn't!*" Elizabeth's eyes were like fried eggs. "I would never go in a store and ask for that!"

"What's so hard about that?" Pamela asked, and we were off again. "Excuse me," she said, looking my way, "but I'd like to buy a jockstrap for my husband."

"Certainly, ma'am," I said. "Regular or reinforced?"

"Steel-belted," Pamela said. We howled, and fell back on the bed with laughter. We even got Elizabeth to smile a little.

When we stopped finally, Elizabeth said, "What I *really* mean is that I'm afraid a husband will think I'm . . . well, too gross, or too messy, or . . . too *anything!*"

We lay there quietly a moment thinking about that.

"When you're married," Elizabeth went on, "your husband sees what you look like in the morning. He knows when you have your period. If you get sick, you even throw up in front of him. It's just too awful."

"Don't worry," I told her. "When you're married, your husband will love you so much that things like that won't matter."

I couldn't believe I'd said that. How would *I* know? And yet, somewhere, deep down, I remembered a woman saying that to me once when I was very small, and I don't think it was Aunt Sally.

It's strange how something surfaces sometimes in your head; you feel you can almost get hold of it, but it slips away again. I seemed to remember, though, sitting out on the back steps with Mother— I *think* it was Mother—crying about something. She had told me not to get dirty, that was it. And I'd gone out in the alley anyway and got my shoes and socks muddy, and when she found me I'd cried because I was afraid she wouldn't love me anymore.

The more I thought about that scene, the clearer it became. Yes, it was definitely my mother, and I remembered hugging her legs as we sat on those steps and telling her I was sorry. She didn't yell or anything. That's the part I remember most. She was so kind about it, that I told her I was never going to leave her; announced that I was never going to get married, in fact. And she said something about yes I would, that my husband would be kind too, and would love me so much that little things like this wouldn't matter.

How could I remember something from so long ago? How could I remember all those details when I couldn't even remember my mother's face? I tried to bring back what she was wearing, or how she'd fixed her hair, but I couldn't. I could only remember her presence.

Pamela had crawled across the bed and was staring down into my face. "Hello?"

"A funny thing happened," I said. "I just told Elizabeth what Mom once told me," and explained about hugging my mother's legs.

Pamela and Elizabeth grew very quiet; I realized that they keep forgetting I don't have a mom. When you don't have a mom, though, you never forget.

Another person who didn't forget was Denise Whitlock, in language arts. Now that we were more or less friends, she'd quit saying things like, "Aw, Widdle Alwice don't have her a mama," and started asking me questions about my family instead.

At school on Monday I happened to mention that I liked the shirt she was wearing, and she said it used to be her mom's, that the only time her mother ever gave her anything was when she didn't want it herself.

"C'mon, Denise. You make it sound as though she doesn't even like you," I said.

"She doesn't. She told me once she should have stopped with five kids. I'm number six."

Different people are bothered about different things, I guess. The reason Pamela, Elizabeth, and I worry so much about our bodies is that we don't have much of one yet; Denise, being a year older, already has most of hers—the important parts, I mean; it was families that worried her—not having one she was happy with.

I couldn't do anything about either bodies or Denise, though, so I decided to concentrate for the next few weeks on my own family—on Dad, in particular. To do all the things for my family that a Woman of the House would do.

"Lester," I said that night, standing in the doorway of his room eating an apple. "What are you going to get Dad for his birthday?"

"Hmm," said Lester, looking up from his philosophy books. "How about a redheaded concubine?"

"A what?"

"Never mind."

"No, what's a concubine?"

"Forget it, Al. Joke! Joke!"

"What's a *concubine*?" I demanded. I hate it when people don't tell me things. How are you ever supposed to grow into a woman if they don't tell you?

I knew he could tell me himself, but Lester reached for his dictionary and looked up the definition: " '1: a woman living in a socially recognized state of concubinage.' "

"Lester!"

"A mistress, Al."

I rolled my eyes. "Be serious; what *are* you going to give Dad for his birthday?"

"Something wild to help him forget he's fifty," Lester said. "I don't know, but I'll think of something."

Lester would too, but I drew a blank. I couldn't think of a thing. Around nine o'clock, when Dad was reading, I called Aunt Sally on the upstairs phone. I figured that someone who had been fifty herself once would know what fifties like. "I wondered if you had any ideas," I told her.

"Can't Lester think of something?"

"You don't want to know," I said. I was even beginning to sound like Lester.

"Of course I do!" said Aunt Sally.

"A redheaded concubine."

There was silence on the line. I knew I shouldn't have told her that. "Joke! Joke!" I bleated.

Aunt Sally cleared her throat to ward off any more nonsense. "When Milt turned fifty, I gave him an electric foot massager."

"Something besides feet," I told her.

"Okay, what about baking him a healthy batch of cookies? Anything made with bran is a good idea."

"Something besides bran."

"A dad can never have too many socks or underwear."

"Besides underwear."

"Well, dear, ask your father what he would take with him if he had to live on a desert island and could choose only one thing besides the basics. Books? Music? Crossword puzzles? Then, whatever it is, buy him more."

"Thanks, Aunt Sally," I said. "That's a help."

I went in the living room and stood behind Dad's chair.

"What is it, Al?" he said, half turning. "I always feel you're going to grab me when you do that."

I moved around in front where he could see me and asked what he would take to a desert island besides the basics if he could only choose one thing. His lips started to smile.

"Besides Sylvia Summers," I said, and we both laughed.

"Black olives," said Dad, and went back to his book.

That was easy enough. I went upstairs and sat down on my bed. I had enough money to buy him several cans. But I wanted to give him more than olives.

I closed my eyes and tried to think of anything I'd heard Dad say that he liked, other than music, which he could get plenty of at his store. Pineapple upside-down cake—I knew he liked that. And then I had an idea.

"Lester," I said, going into his room. "I'm going to cook a gourmet dinner for Dad's birthday."

"Deal!" said Lester. "If you do the dinner, I'll buy the gift, and make it from both of us."

I went back downstairs and got out the recipe box that's been sitting on our counter as long as I can remember. I'd seen Dad use it now and then, but I never bothered to open it. And thumbing through the cards with their worn edges, marked with grease and spaghetti stains, I realized that the recipes weren't in Dad's writing. I was holding cards that my mother had written, cards that she had held, and my heart began to thump. It was as though a little bit of my mother had been sitting there on the counter all these years, just waiting for me to open the box, and I didn't even know it.

My fingers had reached the *P*s, and there it was: Pineapple Upside-Down Cake, it said, in black ink. And over in one corner, beneath a smudge of flour, was the notation, "Ben's favorite."

8

MENDING FENCES

The thing about seventh grade is that most of the time you're sitting around waiting to see what's going to happen to you. While I was waiting to find out what state I would be named after at school, and whether I could go on living when I did, Mr. Hensley, in world studies, gave me a reason to think about a long productive life.

The seventh-grade class, he said, was going to bury a time capsule in the school courtyard. Then they would fill the hole with cement, put a marker on top, and we would all be invited back to dig up the time capsule in the year 2040, when we were sixty years old. Provided the school was still there, that is. If it wasn't, the county had promised, they would move our time capsule somewhere else.

The first part of the assignment was to bring to class a list of ten things we should put in the capsule, showing what our society was like now. We'd list them all on the board and vote for the final ten. The second part of the assignment was to write a letter to our sixty-year-old selves, to read in 2040.

"Sixty years old!" I said to Patrick after school. "That's older than my dad is now! I don't know how to write a letter to a really old person."

"My grandfather lived to be ninety-two," said Patrick.

"What did he like to talk about?" I asked.

"The World Series," Patrick said.

At dinner that night, I told Dad about the time capsule.

"What did you suggest putting in it?" Dad asked.

"A Michael Jackson poster, a coupon for a Big Mac, a . . ."

"McCivilization," Dad sighed.

"What?" I said.

"It's so banal, Al. So superficial!" he complained. "Where are the good books, the great ideas, the music, the architecture . . . ?"

"Hey, I'm only twelve, Dad."

He smiled then. "I guess that's it."

"If *you* had to put in a piece of *your* twelve-year-old self, what would it have been?" I wanted to know.

Dad looked a little sheepish. "Twelve years old,

huh? Well, let's see. That would be . . . uh . . . 1955. President Eisenhower had a heart attack. I remember that because I was delivering papers. I'd put in a picture of Eisenhower, I guess. A picture of Sugar Ray Robinson . . ."

"I'll bet you weren't listening to Bach at age twelve, either," I told him.

Dad gave a rueful smile. "Probably not. My two favorite songs, as I remember, were 'Sixteen Tons' and 'Rock around the Clock.' "

"Gotcha!" I said.

The phone rang, and when I answered, a woman's voice said, "Alice, would you please tell your brother that his sunglasses have been in my car since last summer, and I would appreciate it if he'd pick them up. I'm not about to go to the trouble of mailing them."

"Crystal?" I said. I'm never sure. For the last year or two, Lester has been dating two different women, Crystal Harkins and Marilyn Rawley, and both have been mad at him since Christmas because he can't decide between them. He'd finally started dating Marilyn again around Valentine's Day, but then Crystal was so upset that he sent her a rose, and that got Marilyn mad all over again. I just hate it when they sound angry, though, because I like them both, and would love to have either one for a sister-in-law.

So I tried to keep Crystal on the line until she

wasn't angry anymore. "Crystal, wait. Lester isn't home yet, but I need some advice," I said, and told her about the time capsule. "If you had to list ten things to put in it to show what life is like right now, what would you choose? I'm having a hard time deciding."

"This is supposed to be something that will stay in the capsule till the year 2040?" she asked.

"Yes."

"Lester's car keys," said Crystal. "Then he couldn't go anywhere, and maybe it would keep him from breaking another girl's heart."

I guess there was just no making up with Crystal. But after she hung up, I had an idea and called Marilyn Rawley.

"I need help with an assignment," I told her, and explained about the time capsule.

"You're supposed to think of ten things that are a part of our culture that we might find amusing fifty or so years from now?" she asked.

"Yes."

"Wrap up Lester and stuff him in the capsule, and I'll find it very amusing in 2040," said Marilyn.

I figured my brother wasn't doing so well in the romance department. Did he have anyone to confide in? I couldn't remember hearing Dad say very much to Lester about his love life, and then I realized that was a mother's job, one of those Woman-of-the-

House things. So when Lester got home from his evening class about nine, I went out to the kitchen to heat up his dinner in the microwave.

"Hey, thanks, Al," he said, as I put a plate of ravioli, green beans, and cornbread on the table. "Oh, man. I'm bushed."

He sprawled out in one of the chairs and stretched his legs. "All work and no play makes Jack a dull boy."

"That's just what I was thinking," I told him.

"That I'm dull?"

"No, that you need a little . . . um . . . love in your life, maybe."

Lester had the cornbread halfway to his mouth, and stopped. "Loretta put you up to this?"

Loretta of the Wild Curly Hair runs the Gift Shoppe in Dad's store, and she's been chasing Lester for a couple of months—until we fooled her into thinking that Lester was studying for the priesthood, which is about the last thing in the world Lester would ever do, in my opinion.

"Of course not," I said. "You can do a lot better than Loretta."

"Meaning?" he said, taking a bite.

"I just don't think you're as happy without a woman in your life, and deep down, you miss Crystal and Marilyn and won't admit it. You can tell me."

"It's nice to know you're concerned, Al."

"Of course I am! If there's anything I can do . . ."

"There is. Stay out of my business, okay? If I was really pining away for Marilyn or Crystal, all I'd have to do is call, and I'd have a date for Saturday night."

"Bet'cha a dollar," I said.

Lester stopped chewing. "Serious?"

"Serious." I dug around in my jeans pocket and pulled out my lunch money, laying a dollar on the table.

Lester put a dollar of his own beside mine, then reached behind him for the phone. He dialed Crystal's number first, I noticed, because the last digit was an *0*.

"Crystal? . . . Is Crystal there?" There was a wait. Then, "Hi, Crystal. How you doing? . . . This is Les! . . . What do you mean, Les who? . . . I know it's been a long time. That's why I'm calling; I miss you. . . . Well, I was thinking about Saturday night. . . . You do? . . . The Saturday after? . . . Oh."

And suddenly he was staring down into the receiver. "She hung up on me! She said every Saturday is taken from here to eternity."

"I was supposed to tell you she's got your sunglasses," I said, suddenly remembering.

"She can keep the shades. I'll try Marilyn." Lester paused long enough to scoop up another forkful of ravioli, then dialed Marilyn's number. He was still chewing when she answered.

"Marilyn? How are you? . . ." But when he got to Saturday night, his eyes opened wide and his jaws dropped, and when he hung up, he said, *"She's* going out with Crystal! They're going to talk about me!"

"What did I tell you?" I said, and scooped both bills off the table.

It was then I got the idea; I would secretly invite Crystal and Marilyn both to Dad's fiftieth birthday celebration. Dad liked them, they'd come for his sake, and it would be a nice surprise for Lester. Maybe at least one of them would decide to start going out with him again. I added their names to the list: Miss Summers, Marilyn Rawley, Crystal Harkins, Janice Sherman, Loretta Jenkins, and Patrick (even though I hadn't asked any of them yet). I'd invite Loretta and Janice when I saw them at the Melody Inn on Saturday, but it was time to call the others.

I waited until I heard Dad playing the piano, then dialed Patrick's number and asked if he'd help me make the birthday dinner.

"Sure. What are you going to have?"

"I haven't decided."

"How about filet mignon and crème brulée?" Patrick's traveled all over the world, and he just talks like that sometimes.

"I was thinking more in terms of pork chops and applesauce," I told him.

"Whatever," said Patrick.

The next call was a little different.

"Miss Summers," I said, when my language arts teacher answered. "Dad's birthday is on the thirtieth, and I'm having a dinner party for him. Could you come?"

"Why, how nice of you, Alice! I didn't know you were such an accomplished cook," she said.

"Well, I'm not, exactly, but a friend's going to help me. It's a surprise, though, so please don't tell Dad."

"I wouldn't dream of it. Of course I'll come," she said. "Let me know if I can bring anything."

I put a check mark by Miss Summers's name too. The next calls were the hardest. I tried Marilyn first.

"Did Lester put you up to this?" she asked.

"He doesn't even know I'm calling you."

"Well, for your father's sake, I'll come," Marilyn said. "I've always liked him. But seat me as far away from Lester as you can."

"Sure, Marilyn," I told her.

Then I called Crystal.

"Was this Lester's idea?" she asked.

"No. I've invited everyone I think Dad would enjoy having here. Lester doesn't even know I'm calling you."

"All right, but only because I want to get rid of his sunglasses," she said.

I made check marks beside Marilyn's and Crystal's names.

"Dad," I said later. "Les and I want to celebrate your birthday on the thirtieth, so don't plan to go out, okay?"

"All right, but none of those supermarket cakes, now."

"I'll make one myself," I told him.

I sat down in the beanbag chair in our living room. I was tired already, and all I'd done was the invitations. Now that I was Woman of the House, I'd be doing this for Dad's and Lester's birthdays for the rest of my natural life! If I gave birthday parties, what about Christmas and New Year's? And if I gave Christmas and New Year's parties, what about Halloween and the Fourth of July? How much was I supposed to do and where did it end?

For about the hundredth time that month, I wished I had a mom.

9

WYOMING

~

Pamela got her state on Tuesday. We were just
leaving the cafeteria when Brian Brewster at the last
table yelled, "Hey, you in the blue sweater!"

Pamela turned around. I hadn't realized until
right that minute that Pamela had been wearing a
lot of sweaters lately. Wearing *only* sweaters, practically, since the state-naming thing had started. And
on this day she was wearing a short-sleeved lacy
kind of thing that hugged her tightly, and her long
blond hair spilled down the length of her back.

Pamela turned, of course, and Elizabeth and I
turned too, just to see what the guys wanted.

"Hey, Wyoming!" Mark Stedmeister called, grin-
ning.

"W-Y-O-M-I-N-G!" the other boys chanted.

Pamela's face flushed. She smiled her pretty smile, and we walked on, ducking our heads and giggling, until we were out in the hall.

"Wyoming, Pamela! You got Wyoming! Oh, I'm so happy for you!" chirped Elizabeth.

I mean, all this cheerfulness on Elizabeth's part had to be a lie. Well, half a lie. You're happy for your friend, but at the same time, if you're Illinois, you've got to feel worse knowing that your friend got Yellowstone National Park and the mountains that go with it, and you're still one of the plains.

"I'm Wyoming!" Pamela laughed, her eyes wide open in surprise, as though you had just told her she was Miss America or something. "Aren't you happy for me, Alice?"

"Well, sure . . . of course!" I was thinking what Patrick had told me. "But you're still the same person you were before."

"*I* think you're jealous!" she said.

"Me? Jealous? What are you talking about?"

"Alice, for weeks I've been awake half the night, worrying about which state I'd get, and it's finally happened, and I don't have to worry anymore, and you can't even think of something nice to say!"

Oh, lordy, I thought. "Pamela, it's great! Terrific! Okay, so you're Old Faithful! But I would have gone on liking you no matter *what* they called you. That's all I'm trying to say."

"Oh. Well, now two of us have our states," Pamela said. "After they name you, Alice, then we can start thinking about other things."

And then I knew what was worse than being Delaware or Louisiana. Being nothing. Not getting a name at all. Being totally ignored, as though my breasts were so insignificant that they didn't even deserve Rhode Island.

Dad always says that the quickest way to stop worrying about yourself is to worry about someone else, and when I got to language arts the next day, I saw Denise Whitlock with a black eye.

I could tell by the way she was sitting, with her face resting in one hand, that she didn't want anyone to notice. At the same time, it seemed awful not to say something to her. I realized that I'd seen her sitting this way before, back when we were enemies, but I didn't suspect until now that she'd been knocked around. So when class was over, and the other kids were piling out the door, I leaned over and said, "Denise, what happened?"

"Nothing," she said, gathering her stuff together.

"Yes, it did. Who hit you?"

I walked right behind her as she headed for the door, and when we were outside, without looking at me, she said, "Mom."

"My gosh, what did she hit you with?"

"Her fist."

Why is it always worse, somehow, when a woman does it? Because women are supposed to be gentle, I guess. At the Whitlocks', the Woman of the House uses her fist.

"You going to tell anyone? Report it, I mean?" I asked.

"Naw. I probably deserved it. I was giving her lip."

"Nobody deserves *that,* Denise."

"Reporting her wouldn't do any good," she said. "She won't change. That's the problem—no matter *what* I do, I can't win."

We walked on a little farther. "Some day she's going to feel really sorry that she treated you like this," I said.

Denise gave a little laugh. "Try never," she said.

She glanced over at me suddenly, and for just a moment I thought I saw tears in her eyes, but then she looked away again and shrugged. "It's okay," she said, and turned the corner.

My list of ten things that defined our culture for the time capsule were: a *Washington Post* newspaper article about the old Soviet Union; a Michael Jordon poster; a cassette of O.P.P.; some Nike Air Jordans; campaign literature about county elections; a SAY NO TO DRUGS bumper sticker; a videocassette of *Robin Hood*; a McDonald's Big Mac wrapper; a Jane Fonda exercise tape, and earrings for pierced ears. The problem is that I'm always months or even years behind the times. By the time I catch onto something, it's on its way out.

Our letters to our sixty-year-old selves were due at the end of the month, and I thought I might do better with that.

"I want you to take your time writing them," Mr. Hensley said. "They don't have to be long, but I want you to think carefully about the person you might be at sixty, and see if you can't connect with that self in your letter."

What was amazing to me was that Hensley, who is the world's most boring teacher, came up with something interesting. He probably got it out of a book, but still, he could have assigned us to write about third world trade deficits or something. All his world studies classes were writing letters to go in the time capsule.

"What are you going to say to your sixty-year-old self?" I asked Pamela and Elizabeth at lunchtime.

"I'll ask myself whether I made the right choice—marrying or becoming a nun," Elizabeth said.

"What are *you* going to write?" I asked Pamela.

She was giggling already. "I'm going to put my bust measurement in my letter, and see how I compare at sixty," she told me.

To tell the truth, I was getting a little sick of

Pamela. Wyoming was really going to her head. In gym, she went to the showers for the first time with her towel around her head instead of her body, just like some of the ninth-graders do, just *parading* herself in front of everyone.

"I think she's disgusting," Elizabeth had said. "Alice, can't you make her stop?"

"Did you ever try stopping a freight train?" I'd answered. "You don't have to look, you know."

But Elizabeth had looked. We'd all looked. And I'd realized that Pamela had popped out a lot since we started school last September—a long way from tennis balls, but certainly up to Ping-Pong by now.

"Aren't you tired of waiting to find out who you are?" Elizabeth asked me.

"I *know* who I am!" I snapped. "It doesn't matter *what* they call me."

I was mad at Elizabeth for asking. Mad at the boys for making me wait. Mad at myself because I was mad at the boys. I felt so helpless, so out of control. Seventh grade makes absolutely no sense whatsoever.

"Pamela got Wyoming," I announced to my family finally.

"Wyoming what?" asked Lester.

"She *is* Wyoming," I explained. "Her breast size, I mean."

"God in heaven!" murmured Dad. Sometimes, when he says that, it sounds like a prayer.

"What are you?" asked Lester. "Or should I ask?"

"I'm not anything. I'm not even Rhode Island. I think they forgot all about me."

"I could pick up a West Virginia T-shirt for you to wear," Lester said. "That should give them an idea."

"No," I said quickly, pushing my potato around on my plate.

"A *Virginia Is for Lovers* shirt?"

"No."

"*I Love New York? Ski in New Hampshire?*"

"Les, don't promote it," Dad said. "It's the worst bit of foolishness I ever heard of, and I can't believe that you even care about it, Al."

"That's what Patrick says," I told him.

"Sensible lad!" said Dad.

I kept digging into my potato. "I asked him to name me after a state himself—suggest it to the other guys, I mean, and you know what he chose? Maine. Because his dad took him float-fishing there, and he liked it."

"Patrick just flunked," said Lester.

"But they already had a Maine!" I wailed. "I'm nothing!"

"Al," said Dad, "Your mother told me once that she didn't really blossom out until she reached the eighth grade."

I wanted to ask the next question, but didn't know how.

"Did Mom have nice . . . uh . . . ?"

"Yes," said Dad. "Now quit torturing that potato, please."

I couldn't believe what Mrs. Jones did for Pamela. She went right out and got a T-shirt showing the falls at Yellowstone, with mountains in the background. VISIT WYOMING, it said. I mean, it even *sounded* obscene.

That same day Pamela sat with boys on the bus instead of us. All the way home Elizabeth talked about how sickening Pamela was getting to be. And I wondered if this was the beginning of the end—of us three—our special friendship, I mean. Is this what happens to girls, they get jealous? One of the questions I was going to ask my sixty-year-old self in my letter was, "Do you ever hear from Elizabeth or Pamela?"

10

THE SECRET'S OUT

Aunt Sally called that evening and wanted to know how our "household," as she put it, was getting along.

"Did you finish your mending?" she asked.

"Mending?"

"The last we talked, Alice, you said you were going to go through all your father's and Lester's clothes and mend everything that needed it."

"Oh . . . that," I said. "Well, no. Not yet. I guess I'll start this weekend. I've been sort of busy with Dad's party."

"You know, I keep a list of seasonal things that need doing," she told me, "and when I checked it over the other day, I thought: I'll bet Alice could use this. Now that you're Woman of the House, you know."

"Not officially until my birthday next month," I said. And then I thought of what Dr. Beverly had told me—that you're a woman when you *feel* like one. *Maybe never,* I added under my breath. "Let me get a pencil, Aunt Sally."

When I returned, Aunt Sally began ticking off her list. "Wash windows, inside and out; clean leaves out of gutters; rake up last remaining leaves and sticks in yard; clean out heating ducts; wash curtains; vacuum drapes; wash all woolens and put them in mothballs; dry-clean winter coats; take off storm windows; and commence spring cleaning."

I stopped and stared at the list. It sounded more like a program for a utility company.

"We don't do spring cleaning," was all I could think of to say.

"You what?"

"Dad says Mom never did anything special in the spring."

"Well, far be it from me to tell you what to do," Aunt Sally said, ignoring the fact that she already had.

"We don't have storm windows, either," I told her. "And I wouldn't know a heat duct if it fell on my head."

"They're in the walls, Alice. You call a furnace company to come out and do that."

"Well, thanks, Aunt Sally. I'll pin the list up somewhere."

I was beginning to feel pressured. There was more homework in seventh than I'd ever had in sixth, and each teacher seemed to think that his or her class was the only one we had. Even Miss Summers gave assignments that took up to forty minutes, and if you multiplied that by five . . .

What's weird is that even though she'd been going out with my dad since Christmas, I hadn't told anyone. I was too afraid that they'd start treating me differently, or staring at me in class, or thinking of me as Miss Summers's pet or something.

But on Friday when I walked to the bus stop, Pamela and Elizabeth were whispering over by the mailbox, and when they saw me they stopped.

"What's the big secret?"

"Nothing," they both said together, which meant something too big to tell.

"Come on, what is it?"

"Nothing!" Pamela said again. "Did you finish the assignment for Hensley?"

"Part of it."

"Did you finish the assignment for *Summers?*" Elizabeth asked, and before I could answer, I saw her and Pamela exchange glances.

I stared. "I don't keep secrets from you," I told them.

"Alice," said Pamela, "we just don't know if we should tell you or not."

"Tell me *what?*"

"That's the point. We don't know if we should."

"I'm Rhode Island, aren't I!" I wailed. "Delaware! Louisiana!"

"Not that," said Elizabeth.

I was relieved. Then not relieved. "I've got another hole in my pants."

"Not that."

"If you don't tell me," I threatened, "I'll never tell you if you've got stuff between your teeth. I'll never tell you if your skirt's tucked up in your pants. I'll never tell if . . ."

"Okay, okay," said Pamela. "We . . . Mom and I . . . went to the China Gate for dinner last night, and your dad was there."

I knew before they even told me.

". . . with Miss Summers," Pamela added.

"So?" I said.

"Holding hands," Elizabeth said primly.

"Well, they're both single," I put in.

"Alice, you already *knew?*" Elizabeth said.

I nodded.

"And didn't tell *us?*" Pamela shrieked.

I swallowed. "I didn't . . . I didn't want you to

treat me differently. I mean, no matter what grade she gives me, everyone will say it's because I'm her pet or something. And what if they break up? I just . . ."

That seemed to make it okay.

"Oh, Alice!" they shrieked delightedly.

"Are they engaged?" Elizabeth wanted to know.

"They're just friends, so far," I said. "Well, sort of romantic friends. He doesn't talk about her much."

"It'll be all over school!" said Pamela.

"Not unless you tell. *Please,* Pamela!"

And then Pamela said something very grown-up. "You know, Alice, you're right. The kids *would* think she was treating you special."

Elizabeth thought it over and agreed.

"We won't tell anyone," Pamela said. "It'll be a secret among the three of us."

I put one arm around Pamela and the other around Elizabeth, and wondered if boys ever felt that close to their friends. If boys even gave hugs.

"Patrick," I said on the bus. "Do you ever hug your boyfriends."

"*What* boyfriends?" asked Patrick warily.

"Just friends. Boys who are friends."

"The *guys,* you mean? Do I ever go around hugging guys? Of course not."

"Too bad," I told him.

"You're really weird, Alice. You know that?"
"So you've said."

On Saturday, I went to my morning job at the Melody Inn. For three hours I dust pianos and file sheet music and anything else Dad wants me to do.

Janice Sherman, the assistant manager, usually wears a suit with a scarf and looks like a bank president or something. She once had this big crush on Dad, but he didn't feel the same way about her, so I guess she got over it. She was dating an oboe instructor now, anyway. And Loretta of the Wild Curly Hair used to have a crush on Lester. The male McKinleys always seem to have at least one woman in love with them all the time.

I felt I couldn't invite Janice without inviting Loretta, so I told them both about the surprise party.

"What a marvelous idea, Alice!" Janice said. "May I bring Woody?"

At first I thought she was talking about her cat, and then I realized it was the oboe instructor.

"Sure," I said. "You too, Loretta. You can bring a date if you want."

"I'll think about it," she said. "Will Les be there?"

An alarm went off in my head. "If . . . uh . . . he's not studying or something," I told her.

My first job of the morning was to put stickers on the last delivery of sheet music and then file it according to composer. I was up to the *Peer Gynt* Suites by Grieg when Janice took off her glasses and let them dangle down the front of her blouse.

"Alice," she said, "Woody and I were at the China Gate the other night and happened to see your dad there with a most attractive woman. I was just curious as to who she is."

I decided that everybody in Maryland must have been at the China Gate that night. By the end of May, I figured, half the kids in junior high would tell me that they had seen Miss Summers with my dad.

"My language arts teacher," I said. "Sylvia Summers."

She looked really surprised.

"Really? How did he meet her? At school?"

I wasn't about to tell Janice Sherman that I was the one who got them together. "He met her at a *Messiah* concert last Christmas."

"That's a coincidence, isn't it?"

"Sure is," I told her.

"I just hope he and Sylvia will be as happy as Woody and I," she added.

"They're not engaged or anything," I said quickly.

"Well, neither are we," said Janice.

A second alarm bell went off inside me. I decided

I might as well face the fact that until both Dad and Lester were married off, they weren't completely safe from Janice and Loretta, but I still wanted the two women at the party.

When I was cleaning the glass on the revolving display case in the Gift Shoppe, Loretta said, as she snapped her gum, "Help me choose a gift for your dad, Alice, What do you think he'd like?"

Even though Dad's manager at the Melody Inn, he lets Loretta decide what to stock in the Gift Shoppe. Which is why, along with the Mozart coffee mugs and Bach bookends, we have notepads with "Chopin-Liszt" at the top, Beethoven bikinis, and music boxes with little conductors on top who turn around and wave their arms when you wind them up.

"Well, what did you have in mind?" I asked her.

"We've got a set of jockey shorts, one for every day of the week, with the name of a composer on the seat of the pants: Mendelssohn for Monday, Tchaikovsky for Tuesday, Wagner for Wednesday . . ."

"I don't think so," I told her. "He wears boxers."

"A beer stein with Beethoven on the side?"

"Uh-uh."

We pressed the button on the revolving gift

wheel and watched as earrings, tie pins, and rings came around. I couldn't see anything that would appeal to Dad especially.

"Surprise us," I said. "You'll think of something."

That was my first mistake.

11

CONFRONTATION

~

On Monday, just after I'd taken some books from my locker, I was surprised to find Denise waiting, and we walked to language arts together. It was hard to realize that this was the same person who used to lie in wait for me last semester, bump into me in the cafeteria, or steal my towel in gym—who teased me about my mother, and tried to make me sing the school song. Last semester she'd gone around with a few other girls, but one was hanging out with somebody else, and the other one moved away.

"So what's going on?" she asked, which I've discovered, means, *What's going on in your family?* She likes hearing about the things that Dad and Lester and I do together, just the way a dieter likes to hear about rich desserts. I tried to tell her just enough to satisfy her without making it sound as though we were the ideal family, which, of course, we're not.

"Well, right now I'm trying to get together a surprise party for my dad. He's going to be fifty on the thirtieth, and I'm going to cook dinner for him."

"All by yourself?" she asked.

"Patrick's going to help. He's in my gourmet cooking class."

"Oh," said Denise.

As soon as I said it, I realized she wanted to be included. Sensed it, anyway.

"Do you cook?" I asked.

"Naw."

"Want to help out?"

"Do the dishes, maybe."

"You're on," I told her. And then, my mind racing ahead of me, I added, "Pamela and Elizabeth are going to serve."

As soon as I saw them in the cafeteria that noon, of course, I asked them, and they said yes. I pulled a paper out of my notebook and made check marks by all the names. Thirteen people in all. A gourmet dinner for thirteen. I had never cooked for more than three people in my life.

I called Patrick after I got home. "Mayday! Mayday!" I said.

"What are you talking about? It's still April."
I told him about the dinner for thirteen.
"Mayday! Mayday!" said Patrick.

Elizabeth's mother was beginning to show. Her pregnancy, I mean. I noticed that whenever they walked down the street together, Elizabeth walked a little ahead or behind, so that you couldn't be sure whether they were together or not.

There was no mistaking Mrs. Price was pregnant, though. She's fairly slim, so that when only her abdomen stuck out, you knew it was either that or a tumor.

"It's just so embarrassing," Elizabeth said. "Everyone knows that they did *that!*" "That," meaning sex, of course.

"Either that or a miraculous conception," I said. "Elizabeth, did it ever occur to you that every single one of us walking around on this earth is here because of sex—our parents, our grandparents, our teachers, our dentists. The Puritans, in fact. Even the *pope* is here because his parents did it."

That was a thought that had never occurred to Elizabeth. Sometimes I surprise myself.

"Well," she said finally, "if the pope's parents did it, I guess it's okay. Anyway, Mom's stopped throwing up now, and I'm embroidering a bib. Maybe I'm just a little bit excited after all."

"Of course you are," I told her. "More than a little. I'll bet you're excited a whole lot, if you think about it."

Some people are comfortable talking about sex and bodies and things and some aren't. I wondered what had ever happened to Elizabeth that made her so weird about things. Mrs. Price was very particular and neat, but she didn't seem wacko or anything. Dad says that every so often perfectly normal parents have a child that's more like a little old man or woman, more conservative than either of the parents, and maybe that's what happened to Elizabeth—she got her great-grandmother's genes and chromosomes.

As much as I hated to admit it, though, I seemed to be thinking about bodies all the time—wondering if I even had one. The boys had given all my other friends the name of a state, but not me. I wasn't alone, of course. There are probably a hundred girls in seventh grade, and only fifty-two states, so somebody had to be left out, unless they started calling us Connecticut 2 or Wyoming 3 or something. But it still hurt to think I'd been forgotten.

Only a few months ago, I was one of the Famous Eight. I'd even been featured in the school newspaper. I knew that Patrick was right—it didn't make any difference what the boys called me. But at the same time, I was still hurt. What hurt most, I guess, was that I could be walking down the hall with Pamela and guys would pass us and say, "Hi, Wyoming!" and she'd smile her gorgeous smile. It was as though I was invisible. They missed me entirely.

The next day, Pamela, Elizabeth, and I had just finished lunch and were walking out, sharing a bag of pretzels. My notebook was coming apart, though, so I was lagging behind, trying to get the papers back in the rings, and as we passed the boys at the end of the cafeteria, I could hear them saying, "Hi, Wyoming!" and "Sure like those Wyoming hills." Then somebody said, "Hey, Illinois! How are your riverbeds?"

I could only see the side of Elizabeth's face from where I was, but in an instant it was flaming pink. Her shoulders stiffened.

Then Mark Stedmeister stood up at the table and his eyes were fastened right on Elizabeth's bosom. "Hey, Illinois!" he shouted. "How are your plains doing?" The guys whooped.

And suddenly Elizabeth whirled around and faced him. "Don't worry!' she shot back. "Some day you'll get another one."

I stared. The boys stared.

"What?" asked Mark.

"What's she talking about?" asked Brian, but Elizabeth was stalking angrily toward the door.

"Illinois is a little loony," I heard someone say as I passed, and a minute later I was out in the hall beside Elizabeth.

She was breathing heavily. "I did it!" she said triumphantly. "I said it, Alice! I did it!"

"Uh . . . not exactly," I told her. "You were supposed to say, 'Some day the other one will drop.' "

"It was close enough, wasn't it?" she said, still excited. And then, "What *does* it mean? What will drop?"

"His testicles," I told her.

"What?" Elizabeth shrieked. She went from pink to red, then burst into tears. Pamela and I took her into the restroom and she practically sobbed.

"I talked to a boy about his testicles?" she kept crying. "I can't believe it! Oh, Alice, I hate you! Why did you ever tell me that!"

When I finally got her to stop crying, I explained about the dropping of testicles and how, with some boys, it took a while.

"Listen," Pamela told her. "The guys didn't have the slightest idea what you were talking about."

"They didn't, Elizabeth!" I assured her. "They just think you're a little nuts."

She began wailing again.

What Elizabeth didn't realize is that I would have gladly changed places with her for that embarrassment in the cafeteria just so I could be any state at all. Even Delaware.

To get my mind off myself, I went through Dad's and Lester's closets when I got home and collected all the shirts I could find with buttons missing, all the pants with rips in the seams, all the jackets with a loose lining, and piled them in a corner of my room. There must have been nine or ten things waiting to be mended.

Then I got out Aunt Sally's list of special projects, but the only one that made any sense was washing windows, so I found the Windex and rags. I had a big assignment in math, a quiz in history, a paper to do for Miss Summers, an experiment to write up for science, thirteen windows to wash, not counting the ones in the basement, and when Lester came home, he reminded me it was my turn to cook dinner.

"Just because I'm the Woman of the House doesn't mean I can do everything at once!" I snapped. "Hold your horses."

"My, isn't our Woman of the House in a good mood today!" Lester said.

"Well, if I'm going to cook supper, you can wash some of these windows," I said.

"Hey, what is this? You always cook on Tuesdays and Thursdays, Al."

I stomped out to the kitchen and banged a pan on the stove. When I can't think of anything else to make, I fry some hamburger, boil some macaroni, open a can of tomatoes, and mix them altogether. Then I go down the spice rack and put in two dashes of everything I can find—basil, cinnamon, cream of tartar, garlic, fennel seeds—it doesn't make any difference what. Finally I dump in a scoop of Parmesan cheese.

As Lester watched from the doorway, I said, "I want you to know that what you told me to say if anyone called me 'Rhode Island' has got Elizabeth in a lot of trouble. A boy teased her about being Illinois, so she sounded off, only she said it wrong."

Lester stared. "What did she say?"

" 'Don't worry! Some day you'll get another one.' "

Lester collapsed in a chair with laughter. "Oh, boy! Oh, brother! I can just *hear* the guys after she left! That poor kid is going to lie awake nights wondering, 'Another *what*? Another face? Another nose? A punch in the mouth? Another girl?' "

I decided to change the subject. "Lester, Dad's party is a week from Saturday, and I've invited some of his friends, including Miss Summers."

Lester straightened up. "Sounds good," he told me.

"Do you have his present yet?"

"Ordered and ready to pick up," said Lester. "A balloon ride for two, second Sunday in May."

"You did it!" I gasped. "Dad and Miss Summers!" The whole world suddenly began to look better. "Oh, Lester, that's marvelous! It's so romantic! You're wonderful!"

"I think so too," said Lester.

12

HOUSE GUEST

I spent two hours that evening trying to mend the clothes from Dad's and Lester's closets, and only got two things done. Wednesday, just as I was leaving for school, I heard Dad banging around his bedroom.

"Son of a gun!" he bellowed, which is about as bad a thing as he'll ever say.

I went to the bottom of the stairs. "Something wrong?"

"Where in *blazes* is my shirt with the gray stripes?" he thundered.

Something clicked in my head and I ran upstairs to see if it was in my mending pile.

"It's in my room, Dad. I was going to sew a button on the cuff."

Dad let out a sigh. "Al, if you take something of mine, will you please tell me? I've got on gray slacks, gray socks, and the only shirt in my closet is brown-checked."

"I'm sorry."

"I appreciate your learning to sew, but you've cost me fifteen minutes of searching the clothes dryer, the hamper, and everywhere else I could think to look. I wanted to be at the store early too."

I apologized again and had to run to make the bus. But when school was out, I'd only been home five minutes before Lester came crashing in the front door.

"Who's the idiot who sewed my pocket closed?" he yelped.

I swallowed. "What pocket?"

Lester turned around and showed me how stitching on the hole I had sewn up went all the way through to the back, and he couldn't get his hand inside.

"Oh, *that* pocket," I said. "You could always use the other one, Les."

"Al, I keep my wallet in my right hip pocket. Three times today I felt around for my wallet and flipped because I thought it had been stolen."

"I was only trying to help."

"So what's a little hole in a pocket? Did I *ask* you to mend it? Did you hear me complain?"

I sank down in the beanbag chair in one corner.

"Okay, so I won't mend your clothes. *Go* without buttons! *Go* with holes in your jeans! Go with seams ripped open and the linings hanging out. What do I care?"

"Thank you very much," said Lester, and he went upstairs.

This was a family? I don't know how wives and mothers stood it. If this was all the thanks the Woman of the House got, Aunt Sally could take this job and lump it. I almost called her long distance to say so.

All three of us were pretty grumpy at dinner. We were eating the leftover macaroni, ground beef, and tomato, for one thing. To disguise it, I'd added a can of corn, but it didn't fool Dad for a minute.

"This the stuff we had the other night?"

"Sort of," I said curtly.

He chewed some more. "The spices taste a little strange to you?"

It did taste odd, come to think of it. I guess the longer things sit, the stronger they taste. Actually, the spices were okay—the chili powder and garlic and fennel and stuff. I guess I should have stopped there and not added vanilla too. Sometimes I get carried away.

"Any more complaints?" I snapped.

"Yeah, we could use a little bread," said Lester.

Wordlessly, I got up, took a loaf of bread from the bread box, and slung it on the table, then sat down and started eating again, eyes on my plate.

"What's with you?" Lester said after we'd had sixty seconds of silence. "They didn't name you 'Rhode Island,' did they?"

I didn't answer.

"Delaware? Louisiana?"

"Oh, shut up, Lester!" I said. "I'm not appreciated here, I'm not appreciated at school, I'm not . . ."

"Welcome to the club," said Dad. I guess we'd all had a hard day. More silent chewing. We would have made great actors for the old silent movies.

It was just about then that the doorbell rang. I got up and traipsed into the other room. As I opened the door, I was all set to say, "No, thank you," or "I'm sorry, we're having dinner," when I saw Denise Whitlock leaning against the side of the porch, hands in the pockets of her jeans, shoulders hunched.

"Hi," she said.

"Denise!" I stared. "What are you doing over here?"

She gave a little smile and shrugged again.

"How did you know where I lived?"

"Looked up McKinley in the phone book. There aren't that many in Silver Spring."

I stared some more. "Well, come on in. Have you had dinner?"

"Naw, I'm not hungry."

"Oh, yes you are," I said. "Come on out in the kitchen. We're having leftovers, though."

I led her to the kitchen. Dad looked up, then half rose from the table in greeting. My Dad's such a gentleman he still tips his hat in elevators. When he wears a hat, that is.

"Dad, this is Denise Whitlock. Denise, this is my brother, Lester," I said.

For a moment I was afraid Les was going to say, "*The* Denise Whitlock? Denise 'Mack Truck' Whitlock?" but he didn't. Last fall it was Lester who rescued me when Denise and her gang backed me up against a car and tried to make me sing the school song. I stared intently at Lester, and somehow he got the message.

"Hi," he said instead, and took another bite of macaroni.

"She just stopped by and I invited her to stay for dinner," I said.

"*This* dinner?" Lester said jokingly. "You're kidding. Good luck, Denise!"

She grinned a little.

This time it was Dad to the rescue. "Please sit down, Denise. We'll find something," he said, and got up to open a can of anything from the cupboard.

Denise seemed self-conscious. She sat sideways in her chair, like she was going to bolt any moment.

"Are you in any of Al's classes?" Dad asked.

"Who?"

"Al, that's me," I told her.

"Oh. Miss Summers's class," Denise said.

I heard the can opener going and saw Dad dump something in a pan. Meanwhile I put a spoonful of beef/tomato/macaroni on a plate and added a glop of applesauce on the side, then got Denise a fork from the drawer.

She swung her legs around, leaned both arms on the table, and lifted the fork to her mouth. She took one swallow and dropped the fork.

"What *is* this?"

"Trés mal," said Lester. "That's French for 'You don't want to know.'"

"It would have been okay if Al hadn't put in the vanilla," said Dad.

Denise reached for the water. "Man, it's gross!" She took a long drink.

"I agree," said Dad, and whisked her plate away. "Let's try something else." In two minutes he had a couple of slices of toast on her plate, covered with chicken à la king from a can, with a pickle on the side.

"Thanks," she said, and started to eat.

Dad and Lester went on talking—about the cars, which of them needed oil changes; about who was going to cut the grass this year—and I thought they were extremely rude, acting as though Denise wasn't even there. But as the meal went on and Denise was ignored, I realized she was beginning to feel more comfortable. She even reached for the salt once, even licked the sauce off one finger.

"Dessert!" Dad said finally. "What will it be?" He got up and opened the freezer. "Ice cream! Vanilla and . . ." He started moving cartons around. ". . . uh . . . vanilla and vanilla and . . . Of course! Vanilla!"

And then, as Denise and I stared, he set the ice cream on the counter, got down a box of Oreos, crunched them up in his hands in a bowl, and then added the ice cream and mashed until the whole concoction was gray. It was delicious. Denise ate every bit of hers and licked both sides of her spoon after.

"We'll do the dishes, Dad," I said, trying to think of some way to keep Denise there long enough to tell me why she came.

We kidded around while we put the stuff in the dishwasher. I asked Denise if she was going to eat again when she got home, and she said no, it might be poisoned.

"Did you memorize that poem by Robert Frost?" I asked, figuring maybe that's why she stopped by.

"Uh-uh."

"Want to work on it?"

She laughed. "Not especially. This your house, huh? How long have you lived here?"

"Almost two years. We were in Takoma Park before that."

"Your dad teaches music?"

"He's manager of the Melody Inn."

"Oh." She looked around. "Room of your own?"

"Yeah. Come on up."

Denise really seemed to like my room, which is weird, because after you've seen Elizabeth's room, with her twin beds and white eyelet bedspreads, and Pamela's room, which looks like the inside of a Coca-Cola factory—Coke wastebasket, lampshade, bedspread, and curtains—mine looks like Goodwill leftovers, probably because they *are* leftovers. A twin bed, an old scratched dresser, bookcase, bulletin board with a broken corner, and a folding chair.

But Denise didn't seem to mind that. She was looking at my bulletin board, with the picture of me in Elizabeth's bathtub with bubble bath up to my armpits; the program of the *Messiah*, where Dad first met Miss Summers; the ribbon from around the box of Whitman's chocolates Patrick gave me on Valentine's Day; a picture of me and my mom, when I was too young to remember . . .

I don't know what made me say it; what Aunt Sally had told me about nurturing, I guess—looking out for every member of my family. Denise wasn't even family, but I think I knew what she needed.

"Denise," I said, "why don't you stay all night?"

"Okay," she said, and plopped down on the edge of my bed.

I was pretty proud of my family that evening. I went down and told Dad that Denise had decided to spend the night, and he hauled up the old army cot from the basement. I put my sleeping bag on it for my bed.

Denise didn't have any clothes with her, of course, so Dad loaned her one of his old shirts to sleep in, and Lester found a new toothbrush in the medicine cabinet. But it wasn't until the lights were out that Denise began to talk, and it reminded me of when my grown cousin Carol came to visit, and we were lying in the dark. Somehow it's always easier talking when the lights are out.

"What are you going to tell your mom about where you've been?" I asked her.

"She doesn't care," said Denise.

"I'll bet she's worried. Your dad too."

"I'll bet they're not."

The room was quiet for a while, and I began to think I'd never find out what drove Denise here. But finally she said, "Mom's mad as hornets because she says I took her cigarettes. She walked all the way to the drugstore for a pack, and just because she can't find them, she thinks I took them."

"Tell her!"

Denise just shrugged hopelessly. "She never listens. Get her mad enough, she just starts hitting."

"So what are you, her whipping girl?" I asked.

"Something like that."

"What does your dad say?"

"Nothing. 'That's between you and your ma,' he says. He believes whatever she tells him. I *told* you, Alice, they just don't care. I thought of running away once, but . . . well, where would I go? You know what happens to kids on the streets."

"You can't just stay there and let her hit you."

"I don't. When she's on the warpath I take off. That's why I'm here."

Her thoughts began to ramble after that, and at some point I fell asleep. But in the night, something woke me up. At first I thought it was the sound of a train going through Silver Spring. When it's really quiet at night and the window's open, I can hear the trains clearly. But then I heard something else: Denise crying. Her sobs were thick and heavy, just like Denise is. Gulps, really. This time I didn't say anything; didn't even let her know I heard, because I realized this was her own private time.

Dad, I thought. I love you. And I love Lester. And I love this family, even when we're all grumpy.

The next morning Denise got up and put on the same clothes she'd worn before, ate breakfast with me, and said she was going to walk to school.

I think Dad and Lester and I all realized that she didn't want any of the kids at school to know where she'd been.

"Hey, Denise, I go within a block of the school on my way to the U," Lester said. "C'mon. Hop a ride."

I found out later that Dad had tried to call the Whitlocks after we were asleep that night, but they're unlisted. So he called the police to tell them that if they'd received a missing persons report on a girl named Denise Whitlock, she was safe with us. The police said thanks, but no one had called.

13

CLEANING THE DUCTS

I can understand why Dad likes Miss Summers. At school the next day, she was wearing her hair a new way, curls tossed this way and that, like a tossed salad. She wore a blouse of red and blue and black and green, and a slim, black skirt. She's gorgeous. The only reason the principal hasn't asked her to marry him, I'm sure, is because he already is.

"Why don't you ask Miss Summers to marry you?" I suggested to Dad at dinner, just after I'd buttered my roll.

"Al!"

"Well, why not? She's gorgeous."

"That's hardly reason enough," Dad said.

"It's a start," said Les.

"Well, I haven't known her long enough, for one thing, and she hasn't known me," said Dad. "Can't I just enjoy a woman's friendship for a while without having to plot the future?"

"Sure, Dad," said Lester. "Set your cruise control on twenty and just glide along."

"I'm afraid she'll get away," I told him.

"If she's in that big a hurry to leave, there wasn't enough to hold her in the first place," said Dad.

When Lester and I were doing the dishes later, he said, "I think he's worrying about Mom."

"But she's dead!"

"Worrying about whether he can love someone as much as he loved her. My hunch, anyway."

"He really loved her, huh?" I asked.

"A lot," said Lester.

I was trying to decide how I could help the romance along, and decided that just being Woman of the House would do. The more I could take off Dad's mind, the more he could concentrate on Miss Summers.

So when we got a call around seven from a furnace-cleaning company and I answered, I remembered that cleaning the heat ducts was on Aunt Sally's list of spring chores.

"Just a minute," I said, and went into the dining room where Dad was writing checks at the folding table he uses for a desk. "It's the All-Clean Furnace Company. They want to clean out our ducts, and Aunt Sally said it should be done every year."

Dad groaned.

"Okay, I'll tell them to bug off," I said, and started back to the hallway, but Dad stopped me.

"Wait a minute, Al. This house *has* seemed dusty to me lately. I've been sneezing a lot. Lord knows when the ducts were cleaned last. Maybe never. What the heck. Tell them okay. Make an appointment for some afternoon you'll be here, and have them bill me."

The All-Clean Furnace Company was delighted and said they could do it the following day at four, which didn't say too much for their popularity.

I came right home from school on Friday to be here for the cleaning. I asked Patrick to come over, because Dad doesn't like me to be in the house with workmen by myself. We've got strange heat registers. They're in the floor, and if you want to get warm quickly in cold weather, you stand over one of them and feel the heat billow out your clothes.

While the men went around the house covering up the registers in some rooms and attaching their huge vacuum cleaner to a register in another, Patrick and I sat at the kitchen table to plan what to cook for Dad's birthday dinner.

"What does he like?" Patrick asked.

"Everything. The only thing I'm having for sure is pineapple upside-down cake for dessert."

"How about steak?"

"Loves it."

"Twice-baked potatoes, with cheese and chives, steaks, salad, coffee and pineapple upside-down cake. How does that sound?" asked Patrick.

My stomach rumbled in response. "Sounds great," I told him.

We fooled around with the piano awhile, and then Patrick showed me three things he could do: stick out his tongue and curl it; close each eye one at a time; and wiggle his left ear. I wondered if this was the maturation jump they told us about in health class—a certain time when girls leap ahead of boys in emotional development.

"We're through," a man called from the front door. "You want to sign this, little lady?"

I hate it when men call me "little lady." I took the paper and pen and wrote my name with a flourish. It took up half the page.

The truck was already down the block when Lester came home.

"What the heck was that truck with the bag on it?" he asked.

"Furnace cleaning, Lester. They cleaned out our ducts."

"Oh." He started through the hallway and suddenly whirled around. "They cleaned out *what*?"

"Our ducts. Our pipes!" I said.

"Nooooo!" Lester threw himself out the door, but the truck had already gone around the corner. Lester sank down on the front steps. "My life is over," he said.

"What's the matter?" asked Patrick, following us out.

"My key chain broke this morning, and one of the keys fell down the register in my floor. I was going to fish it out tonight."

"The key to what?" I asked.

"Marilyn's apartment."

"You'd better go home, Patrick," I said. "I don't think you want to hear this."

"Sure I do," said Patrick.

"Mad as she is at me, she never asked for her key back," Lester went on. "Now if she ever asks for it and I tell her it's lost, she won't believe me; she'll change the lock on her door."

Patrick sat down beside him on the steps. "So what difference does it make? If she wants the key back, she doesn't want you to come in anyway. Right?"

"But once she changes the lock, see, then I can't." Lester let out his breath. "And just because she says she doesn't want to see me anymore doesn't mean she doesn't want me to walk in sometime with flowers and surprise her."

Patrick scratched his head.

"But if I lost the key, she'll think I don't care, and if she thinks I don't care, she'll *really* change the lock. Oh man, then even if she wanted me to surprise her sometime, I couldn't." Lester went inside and up to his room.

"Alice," said Patrick. "If we still like each other when we're twenty, and you have an apartment, and you give me a key, and you say you don't want to see me anymore, I'll just drop it in your mailbox, okay?"

Denise hadn't said one word about her mom.

"What happened when you went home?" I finally asked her on Monday.

"Nothing," she said. But I didn't believe her. Sometimes she waited for me to walk to gym and sometimes she didn't. This day she didn't. I wondered what could be worse than getting beat up when you went home, and then I knew: finding out that no one even cared you were gone.

On Tuesday, as I was gathering up my books after language arts, Miss Summers said, "Alice, could I see you for a moment?" All the other kids went on out.

I went up to her desk.

"About this Saturday," she said, and her eyes were smiling. "Tell me how I can help. I'd really like to do something."

"Well, Patrick and I are going to cook dinner.

And two people have offered to bring bread and the coffee."

"A cake?"

"I want to make Dad's favorite. It's pineapple upside-down cake, and I've got the recipe, but I don't want him to know. I'm trying to keep the whole meal secret, in fact, but he'll probably notice all the food in the refrigerator, anyway, after I shop."

"Tell you what," she said, "why don't we make the cake at my house on Saturday?"

I couldn't believe my ears. I was being invited inside Miss Summers's house, to walk on the very floor she walked on and sit in her very chairs.

"I . . . I work at the Melody Inn on Saturday mornings," I said.

"Then why don't I pick you up at noon. I'll be waiting for you on the corner, we'll go do the grocery shopping together—I'd like to help out on the expenses—and then we'll bring everything back to my house and bake the cake there."

"That would be wonderful!" I said.

I wanted to hug her. I wanted to say something so she'd know how much I liked her. I think I loved her, even if Dad didn't. Dad did, of course. At least I think so.

"I'm . . . well, we . . . ," I stammered. "I'm really glad he has you." Then I gulped. I'll bet I'd gone too far.

"Well, I like Ben very much, and it's you who

introduced us, so let's see if we can't make this a good celebration," she said.

After I left the room, I started worrying about what she said, though. She didn't say she *loved* Dad, she said she liked him. She didn't say I'd brought them together, she said I'd "introduced" them. She didn't say they were announcing their engagement, she called it a celebration. Maybe I was jumping too far ahead.

"Lester," I said that night. "If a woman says she likes a man very much, and is glad someone introduced them, and that she wants his birthday to be a grand celebration, does it sound to you like a woman who is thinking of marriage?"

Lester didn't even look up from his magazine. "No, it sounds like a twelve-year-old-going-on-thirteen who thinks she can marry her dad off to her language arts teacher," he said, which is just about what I expected.

14

LOVING LESTER

The closer it got to Saturday, the more irritable I became. There was just too much to do, and only me, it seemed, to do it.

Dad didn't even care that the house had to look nice for the party. Dad didn't know there *was* a party, of course; not that we had invited anyone, I mean. As soon as I picked up one thing and put it where it belonged, Dad or Lester put down another. As soon as I wiped the toothpaste off the sink, I'd find soap stains.

Wednesday I woke up angry and went to bed angry. I'd finally mended all the clothes that were heaped in my room, ironed my best shirt for Saturday, dusted everything that anybody might look at twice, and scrubbed the kitchen floor. But when Lester came home that afternoon, he dropped a box of crackers, and spilled crumbs all over.

"Lester, you pig!" I shouted. "I just scrubbed!"

"Relax," said Lester. "I'll sweep up."

But when I came out in the kitchen an hour later, I could still feel a crunch here and there. I stooped down and examined the floor. Lester had swept a path through the crumbs, from the refrigerator to the sink, but there were still crumbs by the counter and under the table. It was later, though, when I found an apple core on the coffee table, that I went bananas.

"You slob!" I bellowed. "I'm tired of always picking up after you! We just can't live in the same house, that's all there is to it!"

"Oh, shove it, Al! I'm tired of your complaining. Give it a rest, will you?"

I slammed through the house. Went upstairs and banged my door. Then opened it and banged it closed once again. I was so angry at Lester I cried. Just sat on my bed and bawled. I don't know why I did so much crying lately. I think it had something to do with the weather.

It was sometime Wednesday night, about midnight, maybe, that I dreamed Lester died. I woke up sobbing. Guilt, I guess. I was thinking how I'd been living with Lester all these years and his slovenliness had never bothered me before, so why now?

I remembered a letter to Ann Landers in which a man wrote that he and his brother hadn't spoken for thirty years, and then the brother died suddenly, and he no longer had the chance to say he was sorry.

What if Lester got in an accident on the way to the university? What if he choked on a chicken bone at lunch? What if he didn't look where he was going between classes and fell down a flight of stairs? The last memory he'd have of me, just before he died, was of my screaming at him and banging my door.

The problem was, I could apologize all I wanted, but as soon as I tripped over his sneakers again, or found his socks under the table, I'd blow up a second time, or a third. It was too late to write Ann Landers and expect a reply by Saturday.

I got up for a drink of water and paused outside Lester's room to hear if he was still breathing. I know that if Lester had some fatal disease, I'd be as kind as I could to him until he died. So I decided that from now until after the party on Saturday, I would pretend that Lester had only four days to live.

It worked. When I woke up the next morning, I was determined to make his last days on earth as pleasant as possible.

Actually, we collided in the hallway, each trying to get in the bathroom first.

"Go head, Lester," I said. "I'll wait."

"Grummph," said Lester, groggily making his way to the sink.

At breakfast, I watched as Lester took almost all the milk.

"Oops," he said, noticing. "Sorry." He thrust out his bowl toward me. "Here. Take some."

"It's okay," I told him. "I'll make toast."

Lester glanced over at me for a moment, then opened the paper and read the comics.

As he left for classes, I said, "Have a good day, Lester. I love you, you know."

"What?" He turned around in the hallway.

"I just said I love you. Can't a girl tell her brother she loves him?"

His jaw hung loose. "Well, sure. Love ya too, kid," he said, and went outside.

It was working! It was actually working! As I went to the bus stop, I thought how maybe I'd discovered the secret to world peace. If everybody in the whole world went around acting as though the people beside them would die tomorrow, maybe everyone would say only nice things to everyone else.

Maybe I should write that to Ann Landers. Maybe I should put it in the time capsule for Mr. Hensley. What if, in fifty years or so, the world was on the brink of thermonuclear war, and then someone would open our time capsule and there was the answer, on a little 3″ x 5″ sheet of notepaper.

All morning, I tried to imagine Lester in a coffin. There would be a memorial service, of course, and

Dad and I would probably both stand up and say how much we were going to miss him. I swallowed.

"Anything the matter, Alice?" Elizabeth asked me as we headed to the cafeteria at lunchtime. I was trying to imagine that Lester was right at that very moment choking on a chicken bone. He'd be somewhere they didn't know the Heimlich maneuver, and after he died, they would find a little poem in his wallet that he'd cut out from an old Ann Landers column maybe—something called "What Is a Sister?" Maybe one of the lines would be: A rose, a rainbow—a smile, a song . . .

"Alice, what *is* it?" Elizabeth insisted. "You're crying!"

I was? I reached up and felt my cheeks. They were wet. I felt my mouth tugging down at the corners.

"It's . . . it's Lester," I said, not knowing how to explain it.

By this time, Pamela had stopped walking and turned around. "What's the matter with Alice?"

"I don't know. I think it's Lester. Something's happened," Elizabeth said.

"What?" cried Pamela. Now Karen and Jill had come over. Everyone was gathering around me in the hallway outside the cafeteria. This is exactly the way it would be if I heard that Lester had choked to death or gone through the windshield of his car. The concerned faces, Elizabeth's arm around me,

Pamela taking my books, and suddenly I started to cry.

I couldn't believe it. All the time I was sobbing, I knew Lester was fine, but it was all so sad, so real! Just like a movie.

They were herding me down the hall toward the nurse's office, and other kids had stopped now to look.

"What happened?"

"What's wrong with her?"

"Her brother . . . "

"He died?"

"What's wrong?"

"Her brother died."

"He was in an accident, I think."

"Her brother was killed in an accident. . . ."

The nurse heard all the commotion and came to the door.

"It's her brother. He was killed in an accident," said Jill.

"Oh, no!" The nurse pulled me to her and hugged me. She smelled of soap and iodine and White Shoulders cologne. She took me into the sickroom where I sobbed some more, and all my friends waited outside when the nurse closed the door.

She put a box of tissues beside me and sat down, holding my hand. I wonder if nurses know how hard it is to blow your nose with somebody holding your hand.

When the crying stopped, she said. "Honey, how did it happen?"

I swallowed again, breathing through my mouth. "It didn't."

"What didn't?"

"The accident."

"Your brother wasn't killed in an accident?"

"No."

"How did he die?"

"He didn't." I felt like crying again, but for a different reason.

The nurse looked confused. "What *did* happen to him?"

"Nothing."

She leaned back in exasperation. "Then why are you crying?"

"I don't know."

The nurse stopped holding my hand. "Has this happened before?"

"What?"

"Crying about things that haven't happened?"

I shook my head, and slowly, I told her the story of how awful I'd been to Lester all week and about the letter I'd read in Ann Landers, and how I thought if I pretended Lester was dying, I might be nicer to him, and it worked.

She sighed. "*O-kaaay,*" she said. She got up and went out into the hall. "Alice just needs a little rest, girls. She's fine, and so is her brother."

"But . . . she said . . . we thought . . . !" I heard Elizabeth saying.

"She thought so too, but he isn't," the nurse said.

The worst part was that nobody would *talk* to me about it. They sort of talked around me, as though I were still too weak for conversation, and yet I knew what they were thinking. Even when I tried to explain it to Pamela, she said, "It's okay, you don't have to explain."

"But I *want* to," I told her.

"It's okay, Alice."

Leave it to Patrick to break the ice. "I heard you flipped out at lunch today," he said, so everyone would hear. Of course everyone stopped talking and listened.

"I didn't flip out. I was imagining how I'd feel if anything happened to Lester because I'd been so awful to him this week, and it almost seemed like something *had*, it got so real, even though I knew it hadn't."

"Oh," said Patrick. And that's all there was to it.

"You sure caused me a lot of trouble at school today," I told Lester when he got home.

"What did *I* do?"

"Choked on a chicken bone."

"What?"

"I was trying to imagine how I'd feel if anything happened to you, and you'll be glad to know I cried."

"Really? In front of the whole school, I hope. On stage in the auditorium?"

"Something like that," I said.

"Well, it's nice to know I'd be missed," Lester said.

15

TRIAL RUN

Pamela, Elizabeth, and Patrick came over for a few minutes for a trial run.

Patrick stared at the folding table in our dining room, piled high with Dad's books and papers. "Where do you eat?" he asked.

"Kitchen."

"Where are you going to put thirteen people?"

"That's the problem."

"You'll have to serve buffet style," said Elizabeth. "That's all there is to it. Just clear off the folding table and put the food out with a stack of trays at one end."

"Trays?" I said.

"You can borrow ours," she told me.

"Silverware?" asked Pamela.

We went out to the kitchen and counted out enough knives, forks, and spoons to serve everyone.

"Napkins?" said Elizabeth.

It was embarrassing. I didn't know how to tell her that we don't use any, and if we need one, we just tear off a piece of paper towel.

Napkins, I wrote on my shopping list.

"What about appetizers?" asked Pamela.

Black olives, I wrote. *Lots.*

Patrick told Elizabeth and Pamela that their job was to greet people at the door, take their jackets, introduce them around, point out the ginger ale and olives, and start them through the buffet line when dinner was ready.

"That's it?" asked Pamela.

"What do you want?" I asked.

"No band? No dancing? No music? No games?"

"Maybe Miss Summers will think of something," I said.

Aunt Sally called me that night to see how plans were coming. I had to talk on the extension phone upstairs so Dad couldn't hear.

"Tell me what you're serving," she said.

I gave her the menu, and told her how Miss Summers was going to pick me up at noon and we'd go shopping, and then we'd make the cake together from Mom's recipe.

There was a long pause.

"It just doesn't seem right, somehow," Aunt Sally said at last, so softly I almost didn't hear.

"What?"

"Taking Marie's recipe into another woman's kitchen to make a cake for your dad. Oh, I know Ben can't grieve his whole life over your mother, Alice, but I'm always afraid he'll forget her."

"I don't see how he can forget her when he's eating her cake," I said simply.

"I suppose not." Aunt Sally's voice brightened. "Anyway, who all is coming?"

I recited the names of everyone who had been invited, but as soon as I mentioned Janice Sherman, she said, "Isn't that Sherman woman the one who was in love with your father a few months ago?"

"Oh, she got over that, Aunt Sally," I said. "She's dating an oboe instructor now."

"Women never get over a love unrequited, Alice."

There are times I wonder if Aunt Sally speaks English. I'll bet my mom never said anything like "love unrequited."

"Isn't that Sherman woman the one I was worried might sue your father for breach of promise?"

"But she didn't!" I said.

"Just the same, Alice, I think it would make for a happier birthday for your father if she didn't come."

After she hung up, I started worrying whether Dad *would* enjoy the party more if Janice wasn't coming. How could I not invite his assistant manager, though? And was it even possible to dis-invite someone after they'd already been asked?

I imagined calling Janice Sherman and suggesting she may not want to come because we didn't have enough chairs. I imagined her telling Dad the next day that she resigned.

Patrick always seems to know what to do in social situations, so I called him and asked if there was some way we could dis-invite Janice Sherman without hurting her feelings. He said they had an etiquette book and he'd look it up and call me back.

Five minutes later, he called. "Here's what it says," he told me.

In the unfortunate circumstance of having invited guests who would now be unwelcome in your home, or who you discovered belatedly would add to the discomfiture of the others, there is no acceptable way to inform them that they are no longer expected to attend. One would only hope that they would themselves realize the true nature of your feelings, and decline the invitation. In the event they do not, you may wish to cancel the entire event and reschedule it for another day, omitting this time, of course, the names of the now undesirable persons who were invited previously.

"Cancel the whole party and plan it for another day?" I croaked, knowing that if I even made it through the rest of this week, I should get a medal. "Forget it, Patrick. Whatever's going to happen will happen, and there's not a thing we can do about it."

If I had to sum up seventh grade in seven words, they'd be: "There's nothing you can do about it." It's opening your eyes every morning and knowing that a whole day's just waiting to happen and you're going to be caught up in it, ready or not. I could plan all I wanted, but I was stuck with whatever name the boys in the cafeteria called me; I could clean the house, but it only stayed as clean as Dad and Lester allowed it to be; I could play up to Miss Summers till my eyes rolled out of my head, and it wouldn't make any difference as to whether she married Dad or not; ditto with Les and Marilyn or Crystal.

There were problems everywhere I looked, all waiting for the Woman of the House, who wasn't even thirteen yet.

16

RESEARCHING N.C.

Friday began just like any other day. I stumbled out of bed when Dad knocked on the door of my room, groped around in the closet and grabbed whatever I touched first, then tried to find something to go with it.

I waved my hand in front of Lester's face at the breakfast table to see if he was functioning, beat him to the comics, shared a grapefruit with Dad, and changed my earrings twice before leaving to catch the bus.

I sat with Elizabeth and heard her say, for the hundredth time, that she was going to be a nun because she couldn't stand the thought of getting pregnant, but that if she *did* get married, she'd never have children, and if she *did* have children, it would be only one, just to see what it was like. Being pregnant, I mean, not the kid.

Miss Summers looked beautiful in a cream-colored skirt and sweater with gold earrings and necklace, and I wondered how Dad could keep from proposing on the spot.

"She's your dad's girlfriend, huh?" Denise said, before the bell rang. I guess it was getting around in spite of everything.

"Well, they go out together, that's all," I said. I didn't want it to seem like a big thing. "How old do you think she is, Denise?"

Denise studied Miss Summers. "Thirty-five, maybe? No, more like forty."

"That's what I figured. Forty-two, I'll bet."

"How old is your dad?"

"Fifty tomorrow."

"Fifty! He's old enough to be your grandfather!"

I wondered if that was true. Well, technically, I guess. If Dad had married at sixteen and had a son the same year, and the son married at sixteen and *I* was born that year, Dad would now be my grandfather. Of course, if he'd had *me* instead of a son at sixteen, that would make *me* thirty-six years old right now, close to Miss Summers's age. I wondered if I'd ever look like her when I was thirty-six.

"Alice?" Miss Summers was saying, and I realized

that the whole class had grown quiet. "Do you want to start?"

"Huh?" I said. "Oh . . . yeah! Sure!" And I opened my book to read a poem by Robert Frost.

It happened right after lunch. Pamela, Elizabeth, and I were going to go outside and sit on the steps in the sun. We took our trays over to the tray-return window, and started for the door. We had just passed the boys at the last table when Brian Brewster said, "Hey, Wyoming! Hey, North Carolina and Illinois!"

Pamela flashed them a little smile and Elizabeth stared straight ahead, and I took a couple quick steps to keep up with them, the way I always do, when all of a sudden it clicked: North Carolina.

I looked around. There weren't any other girls nearby. Had I heard right? I glanced over my shoulder.

"Hey, North Carolina!" another boy said, looking right at me. "You, in green! How ya' doin'?"

It *was* me! I was the only one in green. I was noticed! Initiated! I was named!

"They named you!" Pamela said after we got out in the hall. "At last!"

"North Carolina!" said Elizabeth, sounding cautiously cheerful.

I tried to think of everything I knew about North

Carolina. I didn't know anything. I didn't even know the capital. Was it flat? Was it hilly? Was it big? Was it depressed?

"Quick!" I said to Elizabeth. "Tell me everything you know about North Carolina."

She stopped to get a drink from the fountain and looked thoughtful. "They grow tobacco," she said tentatively.

"What else?" I pleaded, turning to Pamela. "*Think!* What do you know about North Carolina?"

"The Outer Banks," she said. "I think there's a string of islands or something off the coast. I'm not sure."

We sat down on the steps just outside the front door.

"Hi, N.C.," a guy said to me, coming out. He smiled when he said it.

Was that a smile, or was that a grin? A leer? N.C. That was me now. The way he said it made it sound like "Nancy." Where was it exactly on the map? I couldn't think. *Why* hadn't I paid more attention to that puzzle map Uncle Milt had sent me one year for Christmas? What was it famous for besides tobacco? Did I have tobacco breath, and I don't even smoke? Were my teeth yellow?

"I can't stand it any longer," I told Pamela and Elizabeth. "I've got to go research North Carolina. See you later."

I hurried back in to the library. Patrick was going

down the hall with his drumsticks from band prac-
tice. I grabbed his arm.

"Patrick, what's in North Carolina? Tell me
everything you know!" I begged.

"Cape Hatteras," he said.

"What's that?"

"Some place where there are a lot of shipwrecks," he said.

My heart was beginning to sink. "What else?"

He thought. "Dismal Swamp."

"Patrick!"

"Hey, don't yell at me! I didn't put it there. What's
the matter with you, anyway?"

"The boys named me North Carolina. That's my
name, now. Is that all I am, a Dismal Swamp? A place
for shipwrecks?" I could feel tears in my eyes again.
You sure do get a lot of tears in seventh grade.

"Don't be dumb," he said, and went on down the
hall.

I walked on. Well, *someone* had sat down with
a map and figured out that there was something
about North Carolina that was me. I had to find out
what.

I got to the library and tore over to the reference
books. We have two sets of encyclopedias in our
library, and both of the *N* books were taken. I mean,
is Life out to get me, or what?

There was a topographical globe on the other
side of the library, and I went over to check out the

elevation of North Carolina, but the continent wasn't divided into states, so you couldn't tell where North Carolina was. My stomach hurt. My palms were sweaty.

Anyone who thinks junior high is easy doesn't remember junior high. Anyone who thinks this is the best time of our lives hasn't had much of a life.

Across the room, I saw a guy put down one of the *N* encyclopedias, and I dashed over and took it to a chair in one corner. I didn't want anyone to see me reading it. Didn't want anyone to know what I was looking up, or what I found after I did.

I opened the *World Book* encyclopedia to North Carolina and looked up the section called "Land Regions." It talked about low level marshland, moss-hung trees, the Dismal Swamp, and grassy prairies. And then my eye caught the word *mountain*. It actually said *mountain*! My heart raced.

> The Blue Ridge region is named for the Blue Ridge Mountains, North Carolina's chief range.

Joy in the morning!

> Several mountain ranges make up the northern and western part of the Blue Ridge region. They include the Iron, Stone, Unaka, Bald, Great Smoky, and Black mountains.

I swallowed. I was bald, stone, and smoky? It was all I could do to read on. And then my eye fell on this sentence:

The Blue Ridge region rises from the Piedmont Plateau to heights of more than one mile above sea level. Mount Mitchell rises 6,684 feet and is the highest peak east of the Mississippi River.

I wanted to scream! I wanted to dance! Mount Mitchell was the highest peak east of the Mississippi River, and Mount Mitchell was *me*?

I couldn't believe it! I got up and didn't even think to put the encyclopedia back. I stood straight, head up, chest out, my Mount Mitchells protruding proudly out in front, and for just a moment that afternoon, when I first stepped out of the shower in the gym, I didn't wrap the towel around me.

As soon as Dad and Lester were seated at the table that night, I said, "I'm North Carolina."

"Congratulations," said Lester. "What were you yesterday? Napoleon?"

"It's what the guys *named* me, Lester! That's the state they chose. And Mount Mitchell is the highest peak east of the Mississippi River!"

"I'm glad you're taking an interest in geography," said Dad.

17

BEING MISS SUMMERS

When I went to my job at the Melody Inn the next day, Loretta said to me, "Lie low, Alice. Janice is in one of her moods."

I took the Windex and began cleaning the glass of the revolving display case. "What is it this time?" I asked.

"I think she broke up with the oboe instructor. She asked if I wanted to ride with her to your dad's party tonight, since she would be going alone."

Uh oh, I thought, and realized for the first time that of the twelve people now who would be there, only three were males, Patrick included.

When I went over to the sheet music department

later to see if Janice had any filing for me to do, she was going over receipts. She had on a blouse with a bow tie that made her look like a neatly tied-up package, with all the loose ends, along with her feelings, tucked in. She always wore her glasses on a chain around her neck, so she could pop them on and off when necessary, and you sometimes had the thought that if anybody gave that chain a tug, she would fly into a million pieces.

"Hi," I said. "Any filing for me today?"

"There's some violin music over by the window, Alice. You could start on that. Look on the invoice because there's been a change in price. The stickers are there on my desk."

I set right to work.

"I hope," she said after a minute, "it's not too late to tell you that Woody will not be coming with me tonight."

"Oh, no, it's okay," I said.

There was more silence while I started in on the price stickers. But when I stood up to file the music, she added, "Of course I can't tell your father that Woody isn't coming, since he doesn't even know about the party, but after I get there tonight, it might be a good idea if your father knew that . . . uh . . . well, Woody and I aren't going out together any-more."

In other words, she was available.

"He'll probably figure that out for himself," I said cheerfully, but she didn't answer.

At twelve, I winked at Loretta, then went over to Dad, who was helping a family select a child's trumpet, and kissed him on the cheek.

"Come home right after the store closes tonight, Dad," I reminded him. "I'm baking you a cake, remember."

"Is that a threat?" Dad joked. "Okay, sweetheart. I'll be there."

I went outside and down to the corner where I promised I'd meet Miss Summers, and only waited a minute or two before her car pulled up and I got in.

It had a wonderful smell, and I realized it wasn't the upholstery, it was her. Jasmine or something.

"Hi," I said.

"Hello, Alice. How's it going? Still a secret, do you think?" The car glided out into traffic the same way Miss Summers glides in and out of the classroom at school. She was wearing slacks, with a loose shirt as a top, the cuffs rolled up to her elbows. There were little pleats down the front of the shirt, and she had on loafers.

"I think so. As far as he knows, Lester and I are just having a little birthday supper for him ourselves."

"Good."

When we pulled in the supermarket, I realized that this was the first time we had ever gone out in public together—just Miss Summers and me. And suddenly I wanted everyone to see us. I wanted to find everyone I knew in the supermarket—wanted them all to see the woman who was probably . . . well, likely to . . . well, *maybe* would marry my dad.

There wasn't *any*body in the supermarket I knew, unfortunately. But I kept imagining that people were staring at us anyway, wondering: Who is that beautiful woman with her attractive daughter?

"What shall we start with first?" she asked. "Are you having a salad, Alice?"

I nodded, so we picked out some lettuce, and Miss Summers added fresh spinach leaves. She told me that if I put in some thinly sliced purple onions and white mushrooms they would be beautiful against the dark green of the spinach.

It was the first time I heard anyone talk about a salad as beautiful. But of course, what other kind of salad would Miss Summers make?

Next we chose the baking potatoes, then went to the meat counter for steaks. Miss Summers found some on sale.

Then it was the stuff for the pineapple upside-down cake (I had the recipe in my pocket) and a few jars of olives, some napkins, and ginger ale. . . .

Miss Summers said she'd contribute some Brie, which I had never heard of before, but it was some kind of cheese that looked like it was melting on the inside. Dad had given me money for groceries that morning, and Miss Summers paid for the steaks and the cheese. Then we were off to her place.

We talked about cake on the way—what our favorites are: she likes poppy seed and I like chocolate fudge. In the car, I rested one arm on the window just as she did. I put out one foot in front of the other, as she did on the gas pedal. She tipped her head back a little when she laughed, and so did I. I know that anyone who saw us together thought we were mother and daughter, even though her hair is brown and mine is reddish blond.

Miss Summers's house wasn't exactly the way I had imagined it. I guess I thought there would be filmy curtains at all the windows and flowers in every room, but it was more like a pin cushion. I mean, the rooms were filled with an assortment of stuff— a jumble of photographs along one wall, books everywhere, baskets of knitting yarn with glorious colors spilling out onto the floor, magazines, a jacket on one chair, blouse on another. A pair of shoes lay just inside the door, and she kicked them aside when we went in. I could see off into her bedroom, and the bed wasn't even made. She'd fit into our household perfectly, I was thinking.

"Let's put the groceries in the refrigerator to keep them cold while we make the cake," she said, and pulled out the flour and sugar canisters while I read Mom's recipe aloud. I showed her where Mom had written *Ben's favorite* on one side.

As we were mixing the batter, she said, "What do you remember of your mother, Alice?"

"Not very much," I told her. "I remember some things, but then I'm never sure if it was her or Aunt Sally who did them. A lot of the time I get them mixed up."

"That's natural. You were only four, weren't you?"

I nodded.

She showed me how to add the leftover pineapple juice in place of water in the recipe, and a bit of almond flavoring. We had fun arranging the pineapple slices and pecans and maraschino cherries at the bottom of the pan, along with the butter and sugar mixture, and then we poured the batter on top.

"Your dad is very fond of you, you know." Miss Summers smiled as she ran the rubber scraper around the pan. "This will please him very much."

And before I could stop myself, I said, "He's very fond of you too."

I thought she'd just smile or laugh or something, but instead she grew serious, and that was the only time all day I got a sort of sinking feeling in the pit of my stomach.

"I like your dad very much, Alice," she said. But she still didn't say love, she didn't even say "fond of." And the way she got serious made me decide not to ask her anymore, because I was afraid I might not like the answer.

But maybe that's the way grown-up people fall in love. Middle-aged people, I mean. They start out going to a *Messiah* concert and then they become friends. They get to liking each other more and more, and it slowly turns to love, like leaves changing color on a tree. And finally they decide they want to spend their whole lives with that one particular person. Maybe Dad and Miss Summers were still changing colors.

"I like your house," I told her.

"So do I." Now she was smiling again. "It's just a little thing, really, but big enough for me, and comfortable. All my favorite things are in it; I love coming home at night."

Would she ever love coming home to Dad and Lester and me, I wondered. Coming home to our house? Was it something I could ask? I didn't. I couldn't. I decided that much as I wanted to say, "Please be my mom, Miss Summers," it was part of growing up that I couldn't.

And so I followed her from room to room as the

cake was baking. She showed me the photographs of her sister and her brother's family on the wall in her bedroom, and the yellow sweater she was making for a niece. She showed me the African violets growing on the window sill in her bathroom, and I saw the kind of toothpaste she uses, and her talcum, and the Lady Remington on the top of the toilet. I could even smell the English lavender soap in the soap dish.

I saw her slippers in the hallway, and her terry cloth robe, and the sheets with big orange and green flowers on them, and the chintz-covered chair in the corner with her pajamas thrown over the back, a chair big enough to hold both of us.

Just like she said, it was a comfortable house, and I felt a lump in my throat. I wanted her to be in *our* house. Wanted her slippers by *Dad's* bed. Wanted in the worst way to throw my arms around her and say, "Please live with us, Miss Summers."

What I said was, "I wish I knew how to knit sweaters," and what she said was, "Maybe someday I can teach you," and the "someday" gave me a feeling she was saying, "Someday off in the future when I become Mrs. Ben McKinley," so I let myself be happy thinking about that the rest of the afternoon.

We had lunch while the cake cooled—little dabs of chicken salad on lettuce, and some rolls and jam.

And then it was time for her to drive me and the
cake and groceries back home, and after she'd set
the stuff on our table, she gave me a quick hug and
said, "See you tonight!" and I went upstairs and
looked in the mirror and smiled just like she did—
slow and easy, letting it take over my whole face.

18

Birthday Surprise

I just had time to go over the rug with the vacuum sweeper before Patrick came. Lester sings in the shower, Dad sings when he's making soup, but I sing along with the vacuum sweeper.

I'm not sure why I like to do that, because it's hard to tell which is me and which is the vacuum. It just sort of masks things, I guess. Nobody knows why I was born into a musical family and can't carry a tune, but I get along just fine with the vacuum sweeper.

When Patrick arrived at five, he was carrying a dozen balloons and a bicycle pump. Patrick thinks about things like that. While he filled the balloons and hung them just inside the front door, I cleaned all Dad's stuff off the folding table in the dining room and put it in little piles along the wall. Then I threw a clean bed sheet over the table for a cloth, and put out the plates and silverware.

"I saw your dad with Miss Summers once," Patrick said. "They were coming out of the theater at Wheaton Plaza."

"Were they holding hands?" I asked.

"I didn't notice," said Patrick.

"Patrick, how could you not notice!" I cried. "It's the absolutely *first* thing I would look for."

Patrick stared at me. "Why?"

"Why? Because it would tell me *every*thing! Whether they really like each other. Love each other, I mean. Whether they'd had a good time. Whether they were going to get married, maybe."

"All they have to do is hold hands and you'd know they were getting married?" Patrick said.

"Well, what do *you* look at? What did *you* notice?"

Patrick thought a minute. "Whether they were eating anything, maybe."

"*Eating* anything?"

"And their faces. Whether or not they were eating anything or smiling. Yeah, I'd notice that."

"So were they eating anything?"

"No."

"Were they smiling?"

"Sure."

I felt better.

The phone rang just as we were starting to make the salad.

"May I speak with the woman of the house, please?" said a deep male voice.

Not again!

"This is she," I said.

"This is John Haskell from R.B. Roofing," the man told me. "We were doing some work at your neighbor's today, and happened to notice that the corrugated piping around the distulated chambers of your chimney vents have corrosive seals along the fibularium, and we strongly suggest you replace it immediately."

I blinked. "The what?"

"The distulated fibularium, ma'am."

"What . . . what will happen if we don't replace it?"

"Chimney gas. The entire family could be wiped out in a single night. Not to mention any kind of crawling animal that might be working its way down your chimney." The voice was very, very deep.

Of all times for this to happen! All I needed at Dad's party was a little carbon monoxide or a raccoon coming up through the basement.

"How much would it cost to fix it?" I asked.

"Ball park figure, ma'am, I'd say close to twenty thou."

"*What?*" And then I shrieked, "*Lester!* I know it's you!"

"I can't sell you a distulated fibularium?" the voice asked, but Lester was laughing now. "Listen, kiddo, I'll try to be home by six, but I'm running a little late. Don't hold up the party for me. Just go ahead and I'll be there as soon as I can."

"Oh, Lester, you always do this! Hurry!"

"I will."

I started to hang up. "But drive carefully!" I told him. I didn't want to have to mourn Lester a second time.

We made the salad the way Miss Summers had suggested. We cut the lettuce into pieces, added the rinsed spinach leaves, then the thin slices of purple onion and mushrooms and put it all in the refrigerator to crisp.

Patrick did the twice-baked potatoes. I'd already had them baking for an hour, and he took them out, scooped out the insides and mashed them up with cream and butter and cheese and chives, then spooned the mixture back into the shells again, to heat up when the company began arriving.

Pamela and Elizabeth came over and put the olives in little saucers on the coffee table, and set out plastic cups for the ginger ale. Elizabeth arranged all the silverware into a fan shape, and Pamela did the same with the napkins.

Then it was Denise at the door. She handed me a box.

"Oh, Denise, I didn't expect you to bring Dad a present," I said.

"It's not for your father, it's for you," she told me, stepping inside.

"For me?" There wasn't any wrapping on the box, so I opened the lid. Inside was a signed photograph of Tom Cruise, a bracelet from Hawaii, tiny earrings in the shape of a cross, and a school picture of Denise, taken when she was in the sixth grade, it read on the back.

She smiled a little. "You can wear the bracelet and earrings, and put the pictures on your bulletin board if you want to."

I was speechless. "Of course I do. *Thanks*, Denise! Gee, I feel like it's *my* birthday. How come you did all this?"

"I just felt like it," she said, and went on out to the kitchen with Patrick.

Marilyn came next, bringing a bouquet of flowers and a tin of gourmet blend coffee.

"I parked down the street so your dad wouldn't notice," she said.

Marilyn's hair was long and straight, and she was

wearing a thin yellow dress that I could almost see through if she stood in front of a light or something. I introduced her to my friends, and then she asked, "Lester here?"

"Not yet," I told her.

Janice Sherman and Loretta Jenkins came together.

"We had a hard time getting away," Janice said. "I let Loretta go first, and she waited out in my car. Then I told Ben I had a dinner date, and was leaving early." Janice gave a little laugh and straightened her suit jacket. "I didn't say that my date was with *him*!"

"Is Lester here?" asked Loretta.

"Not yet," I told her.

Then it was Crystal, with a bottle of wine and some French bread. Crystal's taller than Marilyn, a little heavier, and has short red hair. She was wearing green tights and a long white shirt.

"Is Lester here?" she asked.

I wished I'd made a recording. "Not yet," I told her.

She followed me out to the kitchen where I was making more ice. "Who's the girl with the hair?" she asked.

"Loretta Jenkins. She works at the Melody Inn."

"Has she ever been out with Lester?" Crystal asked curiously.

"Around the block and back," I said, which was the honest-to-God truth.

I was about to go into the living room and introduce everyone when I heard the front door open again. We were still waiting for Lester and Miss Summers, so I hurried out into the hallway. There stood Dad, staring at the balloons tied to the banister.

"Dad!" I cried in astonishment.

He turned slowly and looked at me. "I do live here, you know," he said, starting to take off his jacket. And then he saw all the people in the living room.

"Surprise!" they all said.

"Son of a gun!" said Dad, his mouth hanging open, but at that moment Miss Summers slipped in behind him, a small present sticking out one corner of her bag.

"Oh, darn!" she said. "I'm late, then."

"No, he's early," I told her.

"Happy birthday, Ben," Miss Summers said, and moved on out into the living room with him.

It saved me from having to make the introductions. I sort of tagged along behind while Dad introduced everyone to my teacher, and Patrick and Pamela and Elizabeth and Denise watched from the kitchen doorway.

But there were still more footsteps on the porch,

and we heard the front door open. There was Lester, followed by a skinny girl in a short skirt and very bleached hair.

"Happy birthday, Dad," said Lester. "Sorry I'm late, Al. Joy, this is everybody. Everybody, this is Joy."

19
THE PARTY'S OVER

It was the worst party we've ever had. It was undoubtedly the worst party given in Silver Spring all year. It was probably the most awful party that had taken place in the state of Maryland since the Civil War.

Patrick ate all the olives before Dad had even one.

Janice Sherman got a migraine and went home.

Joy, whom Lester had brought because he thought he'd be the only one without a date, turned out to be in the same aerobics class as Loretta Jenkins, and they spent the whole evening sitting in a corner talking about perms and tints.

Lester spent the evening trying to get Marilyn or Crystal to talk to him.

I left the twice-baked potatoes in the oven too long, and when people tried to cut them with a fork, they sounded like glacial ice cracking.

The candles dripped on the pineapple upside-down cake before we could get them all lit.

Loretta's gift to Dad was a set of coffee mugs with members of the New York Philharmonic Orchestra on them playing the flute, the violin, and the cello. When you poured hot coffee in the mugs, the tuxedos disappeared, and the members of the philharmonic were playing the flute, the violin, and the cello in their birthday suits.

We forgot to serve the salad at all.

"It's okay, Alice. The steaks were good, anyway," Patrick said just before he left with Pamela and Elizabeth. Denise got a ride home with Lester and Joy, and Loretta and Crystal and Marilyn left soon after that.

Then it was just Dad, Miss Summers, and me. They were sitting on the couch together, opening the small gift I'd seen tucked in Miss Summers's bag, so I went on out to the kitchen.

Everything looked odd. There were two sacks of trash by the back door waiting to go out; dishes had been put away in strange places. The food in the refrigerator had been rearranged, and the dishwasher was running on the wrong cycle. The dining room looked weird with an empty folding table in the middle of it and all Dad's stuff piled along the wall. There were a few glasses here and there with lipstick stains on them, and the house was strangely quiet.

"No," I said aloud, "I am *not* going to cry. I am sick of crying. I have spent one-half of seventh grade crying."

And then, from the other room, I heard music. It sounded like Miss Summers singing, only I could tell it wasn't live. It was, in fact, Miss Summers singing "Ave Maria," just as she had sung it for me once, when Dad first brought her home and was telling us how the bottom notes of the song were by Bach and the melody was written by Gounod.

I sat very still on a kitchen chair listening to her low mellow voice. When the song was over, there was a pause, and next I heard her singing something else—an old ballad, I think, called "Black Is the Color of My True Love's Hair."

I knew then that her birthday gift to Dad had been a cassette recording of her singing some of Dad's favorite songs. He'd probably asked her to make one for him. It was the only thing that had really gone right—that and the ticket for a balloon ride. It would have been a much better party if I hadn't invited anyone else.

Everything else was wrong, it seemed. Everything in our house was changing, and I couldn't do anything about it. How could I be Woman of the House when I couldn't even give a decent birthday party?

And suddenly Dad was standing in the doorway alone, asking me what was the matter.

"I don't know," I told him. "Everything, I guess."

"Whenever someone says 'everything,' it means one thing in particular," Dad told me.

"No, it's everything," I insisted. "The party would have been a lot better if Mom were here to bake your cake, Marilyn and Crystal hadn't come, Patrick hadn't eaten all the olives, Lester hadn't brought a floozy . . . "

"My word, you're beginning to sound like Aunt Sal," Dad teased, but I barreled on:

"I *can't* be Woman of the House, Dad! I can't be responsible for birthdays and dental appointments and duct cleaning and windows and . . . "

"Whoa . . . whoa . . . whoa!" said Dad. "Who said anything about Woman of the House? This is a family, remember?"

"But Aunt Sally said, now that I'm almost thirteen, that . . . "

"Al, your Aunt Sally's a fine woman, but she's full of asparagus. You know that."

"But she said I'm responsible . . . "

"We're all three responsible. We all three have to depend on each other, and take care of each other. You don't have to do it alone."

I listened.

"All of us are good at some things and not so good at others, honey. Nobody expects you to have the experience of your aunt Sally or the . . . ahem . . . wisdom of your dad. All you have to be is twelve."

He was standing behind me now, massaging my shoulders, and I reached up and squeezed his hand.

"Do you like me?" I asked, playing our little game.

"Rivers," Dad said.

"Love me?"

"Oceans."

I wondered if Miss Summers had gone home, and then, off in the next room, I heard her singing along with her voice on the cassette—harmonizing with "Summertime." It was like hearing two Miss Summerses in one room together, both singing—one in a low voice, one a little higher. And it was beautiful.

We ate "thrice-baked pototoes" on Sunday, all of the salad, and the rest of the pineapple upside-down cake. Dad and Lester and I slowly put the house back the way it generally was; I pinned up the two pictures Denise had given me on my bulletin board, one of her and one of Tom Cruise, and enjoyed being just me for a change. I wasn't Woman of the House or North Carolina, either one.

On the way to school Monday, I thanked Pamela and Elizabeth for helping out at the party, and gave Patrick the last remaining piece of cake that I'd wrapped for him. I wanted to thank Denise too for the work she did in the kitchen, but she was absent.

It was just before sixth period that the principal's voice came over the speaker, saying that all faculty and students were to report to the gym for a special assembly.

"All riiiiight!" Patrick yelled from down the hall. "No algebra! *Yes!*" And he thrust one fist in the air.

I waited for Elizabeth and Pamela, and we all went in together. I looked for cheerleaders down front—a pep assembly—but there was no one by the microphone except the principal and the school nurse.

"What do you bet it's a talk about sex?" I heard a guy say behind me as I settled onto the bleachers between Pamela and Elizabeth.

When everyone quieted down, Mr. Orman began: "Students, I've called this assembly because I want you to hear this from me, not someone else. I believe in telling you things straight, because you are on the brink of being young men and women; you aren't children anymore. I know that when you leave the gym today you will feel far older than you did when you came in. It is my painful task to tell you that one of our students, Denise Whitlock, was killed this morning when she apparently stood in the path of an oncoming train. . . . "

He went on talking, but I didn't hear. I found myself crawling down through the seats in the bleachers, pushing aside people's feet to make room. My mouth felt like cotton, my hands were clammy. Elizabeth and Pamela were trying to hold me back, but I wrestled free, leaving my books behind, and finally dropped to the floor below.

And then I was out in the hallway, gasping for breath, walking with one hand on the wall to hold me up, going nowhere, anywhere.

A second door to the gym opened on down the hall and then Miss Summers was coming toward me. I was in her arms, making strange sounds in my throat, so weird you couldn't even call it crying.

"Alice . . . " Her arms were tightly around me, protecting me against myself.

Something was wrong with my chest. The air was trapped, couldn't get out. Came only in little spurts, a few words at a time: "Her bracelet . . . The t-two pictures she gave me . . . that day in school . . . she had a b-black eye. Her mother did it with her fist. . . . I never told . . . she never . . . we didn't report . . . " I was choking out sounds.

And then my voice turned high like a kitten's mew, and I was crying and Miss Summers was crying. The scent of jasmine was all around me, and

I knew if I asked her then if she'd marry Dad, she'd probably say yes. Yes to anything. I also knew that Mr. Orman was right; I was a lot older now than when I'd entered the gym, and everything that had happened before seemed light-years away from what was happening now. So I just kept on crying. April was the month of tears.

Miss Summers drove me home. She stayed awhile, then Dad came and she left. They said all the right things—how no one knew just how bad things were going for Denise; how sometimes you can tell when someone's thinking about suicide and sometimes you can't; how nice it was that I had befriended her, and the fact that she'd given me some favorite things showed how much that friendship meant.

But it hadn't meant enough to save her. If I'd known Denise better, I might have known what her giving me that stuff really meant. I might have talked her out of it. All the time we were eating pineapple upside-down cake the night of the party, Denise had probably known what she was going to do come Monday.

"The . . . the thing is," I said to Dad, "she . . . wasn't really a *friend*. Not a close one, I mean. In a lot of ways I didn't even like her. I was just nice to her."

"You can't *make* yourself like someone, Al."

"Why did she *do* it? There were people she could have talked to about it. Someone would have helped her. Once she . . . once she decided to kill herself, she didn't have any choices left."

"I don't know why, Al. None of us really knows what it was like to be Denise."

Things were real quiet around school that week. Kids didn't do a lot of laughing, especially the day of the funeral. A lot of us stopped in on our way home from school Wednesday to sign the register. The coffin was closed. I couldn't tell from the various relatives who the parents were. Some of them were crying; some weren't. A rumor went around that social workers placed some of the Whitlock kids in foster homes, but I don't know if it was true or not.

Pamela, Elizabeth, and I got together every evening and talked. At Pamela's, her mother made chocolate chunk cookies the size of saucers, as though cookies would help pull us through. If only they would have helped Denise. If it were just that simple.

It helped to have friends to share feelings with, though. No matter what our parents said, no matter how logical their arguments, we kept asking, "What if . . . ?" No matter how we tried not to think about it, our thoughts returned again and again to those railroad tracks, and what Denise must have been feeling when she headed there instead of school on Monday. And then . . . the thought of the train coming . . . of Denise just standing there . . . the engineer blowing the whistle . . . Denise just standing. . . .

I couldn't seem to stop shivering.

"We've got to promise," Elizabeth said tearfully, "that if any of us ever, *ever* thinks about doing something like that, she'll tell the others."

"What if she can't?" asked Pamela. "What if all she knows is she's depressed, and she doesn't think about killing herself till five seconds before she decides to do it?"

"There are signs," I said. "Like if one of us cries all the time. . . . "

"We *all* cry all the time!" said Elizabeth. "I've cried more since I got to seventh grade than I ever did in my life."

"Okay, scratch crying," I said. "If one of us starts giving away her stuff, then we worry."

Pamela thoughtfully chewed her lip. "What about those earrings you gave me last month, Alice? You said you didn't want them anymore."

"One pair doesn't count," I said. "Two pairs, a warning sign. Three mean business."

"And if one of us talks a lot about dying, that would be a sign," Elizabeth said.

"It doesn't count, though, if someone says, 'I'll

just die!' " I told them. "Elizabeth says that once a day."

"Okay, it's serious if one of us really makes plans," Pamela decided.

We were lying side by side on Pamela's bed, picking cookie crumbs off the spread, and finally Pamela turned over and said, "You know what? When you come right down to it, all we can do is just try to be the best friends to each other that we can and hope it's enough."

Elizabeth sniffled a little. I think I was sniffling too.

"You're right," I said, my nose all clogged. "Our parents have been alive a lot longer than we have and they don't have all the answers either."

Maybe that was it. You just try to be the best twelve you can be or the best thirty or the best seventy—whatever age you are—and then, whatever you have, you run with it.

"I feel like I want to do something for Denise, though," I told them. "We talked about it in Hensley's class today. Somebody said we should put the newspaper article about her death in the time capsule, and maybe a poem about her or something; give her a little immortality, but Hensley said no."

"That's what he told our class too," said Elizabeth. "He said we had to think about what kind of a signal we were sending if we give Denise all the fame and attention in death that she missed in life."

And so, when the time capsule was buried on Friday, with all our letters in it, our school pictures, and the ten objects we'd voted on in class, there was no newspaper story of Denise's death. But Mr. Hensley let me, by special request, place Denise's bracelet from Hawaii in the capsule so that when we opened it in the year 2040, I'd find a private memento, from Denise to me, of a girl I hardly knew.

20

A LETTER TO MYSELF

On Sunday, Dad and Miss Summers went up in the hot air balloon.

We'd all got up at four in the morning, and Lester and I drove them to a field in Virginia where the balloons were launched. Dad had brought a bottle of champagne to take with them, Miss Summers packed a lunch, and she was more giggly than I'd ever seen her before. I think maybe she was a little nervous. Maybe even a little scared. It's weird to think about your teacher being scared. This time she was wearing jeans and a cotton sweater.

No one knew exactly where the balloon would land, so a chase car always followed them from below. Once the balloon came down, the driver brought them to a parking lot about fifteen miles away, where we were going to wait for them. But they were twenty feet up in the air when Lester realized that Dad had his car keys. After Dad had taken Miss Summers's lunch out of the trunk, he'd forgotten to give the keys back.

We were both yelling and jumping up and down.

"Dad!" Lester bellowed. "The keys! My car keys!"

Dad's face froze for a moment, and then he jerked his hand in his pocket and threw the keys over the side of the balloon. Lester went scrambling through the grass after them, and the last I saw of Miss Summers, her head was tilted back in laughter and her hair was blowing in the wind. Just like in the shampoo commercials.

We walked back to the car, Les and I. It was an almost perfectly quiet morning. Mist was still rising up over the fields, and even though the wind was chilly, the sun was warm—the kind of day you just know can only get better.

"And so they lived happily ever after," I said.

"Who?"

"Dad and Miss Summers. Do you think they'll marry, Lester?"

"Who knows? But *no*body lives happily ever after, Al. A lot of the time, maybe, but not all the time. Not even language arts teachers."

We got in the car, and Lester started the engine.

I guess I was having trouble giving up being Woman of the House, because I heard myself asking, "Did you ever make up with Marilyn or Crystal?"

"Make up as in 'happily ever after'?" Lester asked.

"No, as in talking on the phone now and then," I told him.

Lester nodded. "It's Joy who's upset. She said I spent the whole evening making eyes at old girlfriends while she got stuck with Loretta."

"So now Joy's mad at you?"

"Not anymore. I sent her a rose."

I groaned, but Lester had turned on the radio, and didn't notice. I knew if I said anymore, I'd have to shout, so I stretched out my legs and prepared to enjoy the ride.

As I thrust my hands in my pockets, my fingers touched a piece of paper. I pulled it out, unfolded it, and found the draft of the letter I had turned in to Hensley to go in our time capsule:

Letter to Myself

Dear Alice:

I can't believe that when you read this you'll be sixty years old. Right now that seems ancient to me—

older than Dad, even. I wonder if you feel ancient inside or if you still feel like you always did.

Dad will be gone, of course, by the time you get this letter. Maybe Lester too, and it's hard for me to even write about that. But maybe you'll be married and have children and grandchildren, and when you do, I guess that makes up for the people you lose. Does it? A little, even?

What I want to know is how your life has been so far, and what you decided to be. Did you ever get breasts as big as tennis balls, and was it still important to you when you did? Do you still have any red in your hair, or is it all gray? Are you fat? Do you wear orthopedic shoes? Can you still wear shorts in the summertime?

Is your favorite food still fried onion rings? Is your favorite color still green? Does the name "North Carolina" ring any bells? Do you ever hear from Elizabeth or Pamela? Whatever happened to Patrick?

Maybe what I really want to know is, did you ever reach an age where you could forget all the stupid, ridiculous things you've done and said, or do you still wake up in the middle of the night and remember each one exactly, embarrassing you all over again?

Maybe you're a famous chef by now. Or maybe you stay home and feed your cats. But whatever you are, I hope you never forget me, the girl I am now.

Love,
Alice

EMBARRASSMENT.

You know how it feels.

These days that's all Alice is suffering.
Instead of growing up, she seems to be growing backward!

HAVE *YOU* EVER

Yes No

☐ ☐ · opened a dressing room door on a boy, or done
           something equally embarrassing?
☐ ☐ · been the one who gets the totally uncool
           teacher?
☐ ☐ · had a disastrous Valentine's Day?
☐ ☐ · not known you have a terrible stain on your
           shirt?

All of these EMBARRASSING events
have happened to Alice.

If you've missed any of them,
now's the time to catch up.

Read:

The Agony of Alice

How will Alice McKinley grow up to be a normal
teenager when she has no role model? Her mother is
dead, so that leaves Alice's dad to go clothes shopping
and pick out a horrible pair of jeans for her.

The beautiful sixth-grade teacher, Miss Cole, would be
a perfect mother substitute for Alice. Too bad Alice is
stuck with plain Mrs. Plotkin. . . .

Alice in Rapture, Sort Of

It's the summer before junior high, and Alice and her best friends Elizabeth and Pamela are convinced that they need boyfriends to be successful in school.

Luckily, Alice has Patrick, who has always been a good friend, but how will he rate as a boyfriend? And just what are the rules of dating and kissing??? Alice can't ask her dad!

Reluctantly Alice

After her first day in junior high, Alice can think of at least seven things about seventh grade that stink. After a week, Alice decides maybe junior high isn't so bad. That's before she has her first run-in with Denise "Mack-Truck" Whitlock.

Alice has survived plenty of problems before, but this one's a whopper!

All but Alice

There are, Alice decides, 272 horrible things left to happen to her in her life, based on the number of really horrible things that have happened already. And she's only just started seventh grade.

Alice joins the All-Stars Fan Club and the earring club and becomes one of the popular Famous Eight. But how should she act when her father dates her teacher, Miss Summers? And how do you accept a box of valentine candy from a boy???

Alice in April

When Aunt Sally reminds her that she'll soon be thirteen and the Woman of the House, Alice starts to worry. Her father's fiftieth birthday is coming up. Does that mean she has to plan the party? And make sure that everyone in her family gets a physical? That means Alice herself will have to take off her clothes at the doctor's! Then there's the latest crisis in school, where a group of boys have begun to match each girl with the name of a state—mountains or no mountains....